When the Whales Leave

When the Whales Leave

Yuri Rytkheu

Translated from the Russian by

Ilona Yazhbin Chavasse

MILKWEED EDITIONS

The characters and events in this book are fictitious. Any similarity to real persons, living or dead, is coincidental and not intended by the author.

Published 2019 by Milkweed Editions
Printed in the United States of America
Cover design and illustration by Mary Austin Speaker
19 20 21 22 23 5 4 3 2 1
First Edition

Milkweed Editions, an independent nonprofit publisher, gratefully acknowledges sustaining support from the Alan B. Slifka Foundation and its president, Riva Ariella Ritvo-Slifka; the Ballard Spahr Foundation; *Copper Nickel*; the Jerome Foundation; the McKnight Foundation; the National Endowment for the Arts; the National Poetry Series; the Target Foundation; and other generous contributions from foundations, corporations, and individuals. Also, this activity is made possible by the voters of Minnesota through a Minnesota State Arts Board Operating Support grant, thanks to a legislative appropriation from the arts and cultural heritage fund. For a full listing of Milkweed Editions supporters, please visit milkweed.org.

Library of Congress Cataloging-in-Publication Data

Names: Rytkhêu, Yurii 1930-2008, author. | Chavasse, Ilona Yazhbin, translator.
Title: When the whales leave / Yuri Rytkheu ; translated from the Russian by Ilona Yazhbin Chavasse.
Other titles: Kogda kity ukhodiat. English | Seedbank (Minneapolis, Minn.)
Description: Minneapolis : Milkweed Editions, 2019. | Series: Seedbank; 3 | Summary: "a vibrant retelling of the origin story of the Chukchi, a timely parable about the destructive power of human ego"-- Provided by publisher.
Identifiers: LCCN 2019022510 (print) | LCCN 2019022511 (ebook) | ISBN 9781571311313 (paperback) | ISBN 9781571317254 (ebook)
Subjects: LCSH: Chukchi--Fiction. | Chukchi Peninsula (Russia)--Fiction. | Whales--Fiction.
Classification: LCC PG3476.R965 K613 2019 (print) | LCC PG3476.R965 (ebook) | DDC 891.73/44--dc23
LC record available at https://lccn.loc.gov/2019022510

Milkweed Editions is committed to ecological stewardship. We strive to align our book production practices with this principle, and to reduce the impact of our operations in the environment. We are a member of the Green Press Initiative, a nonprofit coalition of publishers, manufacturers, and authors working to protect the world's endangered forests and conserve natural resources. *When the Whales Leave* was printed on acid-free 30% postconsumer-waste paper by Sheridan Books, Inc.

Contents

Yuri Rytkheu was born in 1930 in Uelen, a small town on a long, narrow barrier spit perched between a lagoon and the Bering Sea. The northeastern coast of Chukotka is raw, cold, and remote, though it's only sixty-one miles across the ocean to Wales, Alaska. On both the Russian and American sides, life has been dedicated to bowhead whale hunting for thousands of years.

In those places the whale is at the center of existence, nutritionally and spiritually. The animals are hunted from traditional walrus hide boats in dangerous spring ice and after, celebrations, clearing out of meat storehouses, and sacred dances are performed in the *qasiq* (dance hall) as an expression of gratitude when a whale has given itself to a hunting crew.

Yuri was the son of a hunter and the grandson of a local shaman. He earned money for university out on the ice and on the sea as a stevedore. He witnessed the decline of traditional lifeways and the ways that both communism and an open market economy dismembered the cultural threads that held a subsistence hunting society together. He remembered "whale temples"—colonnades of whale jaws and ribs lining the shores of the peninsula. He remembered the fickle currents and winds that quickly moved pack ice and brought migrating whales nearby. He remembered stories of the epidemics brought by European whalers that eviscerated whole villages, and the over-harvesting of whales and walruses by outsiders for profit in the midst of subsistence hunting territory. He understood that as soon as you have to leave the village to work for a wage, traditional culture falls apart. He understood the necessity of holding the whole culture in your mind and heart, that if you don't, the center won't hold.

When the Whales Leave is a spare, three-part, generation-spanning novel that begins in what Arctic people call "ancestor times": when animal-human transformations were common; when time and lifespans were elastic; when the world was densely populated not with humans, but with stars, mountains, ice floes, animals, birds, fish, plants, rocks; when personhood was observable everywhere.

Nau is a young woman who falls in love with a whale who, smitten with love, becomes a man so he can live with her. She is a perpetrator of and participant in the creation of earth, and she helps people it. Passing whales beckon her, she feels an irresistible tug, one that is urgent and sexual, and after falling in love with Reu, the whale-man, she gives birth to whale-children, nurses them at the shore, and later is the mother of human children. Reu provides for them—not whale meat but caribou. As the children grow, Nau becomes First Mother, dispensing wisdom and admonitions, then an elderly pest who bums around the village staying with whoever will let her in.

When the son who questions his mother's creation story is lost with his whaling crew in bad ice and faces certain death, he is astonished when whales rescue them and bring them ashore. Another son becomes curious and takes others with him on a long journey to see the world, a trip that takes nearly a lifetime. The next generation stays at home but questions the usefulness of traditional lifeways and the veracity of the legends Nau tells him. And on it goes, a tracery of the vertiginous fall from tradition, from moral rectitude and its consequences.

Yuri lived the fall: this novel is a tribute to the relevance of the old ways that have been trampled and disposed of. The scale is intimate and concise—almost translucent—befitting the language of those who recount legends. He follows the downward spiral from respect for the power of the natural world, modesty in front of the weather, and group effort, to the generational shift that produced, finally, a vain bully and gloating brute whose final murderous acts kill the long-lasting First Mother, Nau.

It is an old story and a modern story, and above all, a cautionary tale. Though originally published in 1975, it is evermore relevant today. Yuri's Chukchi name "Rytgev," means "forgotten." It's hard to know the sense behind it, but in my mind, his name has come to stand for the hard-won and thoughtful way Arctic people behave and the dismissive way in which they are regarded in the modern world. I know because I've traveled with subsistence Inuit hunters in Greenland by dogsled for twenty-five years.

Arctic people evolved with ice. For them, weather is consciousness. Self-discipline, perseverance, modesty, and generosity are the necessary survival tools in a harsh world that is light for six months and dark for the other six, where death comes easily and often, where chance and transience and a robust humor are vital to how they live in the world.

So much of that 30,000-year-old Arctic culture has been desecrated culturally as well as biologically, even as our anthropocentric trajectory toward extinction escalates. It must have been heartbreaking for Yuri, who died in 2008. To stem those losses, urgently felt in his St. Petersburg home, the novel stands as a renewal of faith in his Chukotka homeland. It is a song that celebrates, illuminates, warns, and finally exposes what were once the moral principles of village life that were traded down for the furious power-mongering and "me-ism" of today.

Every element of *When the Whales Leave* is based on legends that have been carried from the northeastern coast of Siberia across the Bering land bridge all the way to Greenland—from Vankarem to Siorapaluk—and are still told today. The migration trail of indigenous people across the polar north took them to the top of Alaska, through the MacKenzie Delta, the archipelago of Nunavut, then across the Smith Sound to Etah, Greenland—a well-used route taken by dogsled that is now callously referred to as the "Northwest Passage."

Yuri Rytkheu applied to the prestigious Institute of the Peoples of the North and when he failed to get in, he studied literature at Leningrad State University (now Saint Petersburg State University). St Petersburg is famous for ethnography and Yuri was fascinated by the ethnographic efforts of Vladimir "Tan" Bogoraz, who died when Yuri was six, plus the traditional ecological knowledge imparted to him by his own family.

In Arctic literature there are hundreds of creation stories, and charmingly, Yuri composed his own. The woman, Nau, existed; the power of love caused a whale to become human, and the desire to communicate resulted in the birth of language. "It was through me that land and the sea joined, through my body that human beings were born," Nau says. Ageless, Nau becomes a Greek chorus of one: witnessing, celebrating, dispensing wisdom and warnings, whether or not anyone listens. Ordinary and wise, she is central and peripheral at the same time, and, roaming from house to house, she sees all.

"Whales have ears and are like people," one old woman said. In the old days differences between humans and animals were porous and permeable. Across the polar north it was known that whales and bears could understand what humans said, that any animal could marry any human and vice versa: a chief's son married a bear, a girl eaten by wolves becomes a caribou, a hunter is lured by a woman who turns out to be a night owl, a seal's soul is revealed inside a dancer's mask, the soul of an animal killed its killer because it was not cut up tenderly.

Tales of world journeys were common. People were said to take off and stay gone for lifetimes. They left young and came back unrecognizably old. Shamans who were tied up facing the wall of a house were able to fly through sod, ice, and mountains; heal the sick; and find lost things.

Time had no chronological scaffold: no one was keeping time, nor did they seem to notice gravity. Everything was alive, and there was an uncanny liveliness in people's sense of themselves.

A few weeks ago, I spent time on a remote barrier island twenty-five miles off the coast of Utqiagvik and I couldn't help thinking of Uelen. How quickly its borders are eroding, intruded upon by raging Arctic seas that, without the calming lid of ice, have become dark and violent heat sinks. Villagers, seabirds, polar bears, seals, and walruses are compelled to find new places to live as sea ice disappears, and the very bits of land—barrier islands and long spits of stone, gravel, and sand—will soon be washed away by rising waters. Those who have failed to consider the whole, the health of language and lifeways as well as biological diversity, and who have strived solely for profit are now reaping the consequences as land and sea ice are pulled out from under us all. How lucky we are to have Yuri Rytkheu's transcendent work of literature. May it save our lives.

-GRETEL EHRLICH
MELVILLE, MONTANA, 2019

When the Whales Leave

Part I

1

Nau loved the sight of the bright, shimmering gusts as they sprang up suddenly over the sea; sparkling jets of water leaping high in the air, with the sun riffling through them, weaving in glittering rainbows.

Nau ran barefoot over the cool, damp grass. When beach shingle tickled her feet, the girl's soft laughter mingled with the clinking of the sea-smoothed pebbles as they rolled about in the surf.

Nau was fast breeze, green grass, wet shingle, high cloud, and endless blue sky, herself and all these things at once.

And when startled birds, and arctic squirrels, and stoats, gray in their summer coats, scattered from her path, Nau called out to them full throated with joy, and the creatures understood her. They watched her as she passed, the tall maiden with long, streaming hair, black as wings.

She had never yet thought of herself as separate from those who dwelled in ground warrens, or nested on cliffs, or crawled in the grass, nor thought of herself as different from them. Even the sullen black rocks were alive and dear to her.

She looked upon all these things with the same serene goodwill: the living things that each had voice and cry, the silent things that nevertheless moved, and the things that were at rest eternally.

And so it went with her until the first time she noticed the whale spout approaching the shore, so high and so strident— until she gazed at last on the long, taut, shining body of the sea giant Reu.

The whale drew ever closer, until she could hear the shingle creak under his weight. The cold wave that preceded his bulk stung Nau's bare feet like a burn.

At first the girl was careful not to come too near. Something powerful and forbidding moved in her when she came down to the shoreline, the place where dried-out seashells would crumble from the slightest touch, and where pieces of bark and even whole dead tree trunks lay strewn about, preserved in salt water.

Nau observed the whale from afar and, seeing how his gigantic black body mirrored the sun's bright rays, imagined the whale glowing from within.

Water rushed into his great mouth with a burbling murmur, sieving tiny seashells and jellies; the watery spray above his head made rainbows.

She longed to come closer—against the silent prohibition, across the unspoken threshold marked by a line of washed-up colored shingle. She wanted to touch the gleaming mist, to feel on her skin even just one of those droplets, each shining with a tiny sun.

One day she crept so near the whale that the fountain he made drenched her from head to foot.

It was both unexpected and somehow familiar, just as she had imagined it would be. The water was warm and full of light, the sun's rays stroked her skin, and Nau felt a new and unfamiliar sense of tenderness, a kind of catch in her breast. She was panting and slightly dizzy, like when she sat too long atop a high cliff watching cloud shadows skitter across the sea.

But the whale went on caressing her body with gentle, sun-drenched pulsing and her ears with the quiet ripple of coursing water.

Nau felt her heart expanding, filling her chest and making it hard to breathe. Her blood warmed with the heat of the whale's pulsing jets, and she stood as in a trance, unsure of what to do. Before, she did not hesitate. . . . she had been as the wind, the waves, the clouds, the growing grass and hidden flowers, the squirrels and birds on the wing, the beasts and fishes that swam in the sea. She had been a part of the huge world that was both alive and dead, gleaming and lost in shadows, lulled to sleep by the domed silent sky and the coverlet of soft clouds, or else raging, as when a sudden hurricane rocked the waves and flung them onto the shore, coursing toward Nau's feet, which were always cold, try as she might to warm them in the grass.

Something different coursed through her now. It was as though she had just opened her eyes from sleep, but the moment of awakening went on and on—as though she was seeing the sky and blue sea and green grassy hills for the first time, and hearing anew the squeaking of the gopher, the ringing birdsong over the cliffs, the murmuring of the stream . . . as though she was discovering for the first time that seawater tastes differently than water from the brook, or that the morning's chill vanishes as the sun rises over the sea.

Later, when she passed through the tundra with her quick, springing step, she took time to peer at the tiny blue flowers that dotted the grass like slivers of sky. The little blue eyes trembled on their thin green stalks, and Nau could hear their piercing, evanescent chiming.

The world of sound gave up its mysteries to her as had the world of sight, and now she knew whence came the thundering waves that beat against the crags, the whistling of the wind as it smoothed the tundra grasses with a vast open hand, the splashing of the small waves in the lagoon, the babbling of the brook as it ran down a rocky slope.

The talk of the birds and the beasts, too—she knew now the language of each.

The black raven croaked black sounds, and these sounds were dark and cold, like the shadows on the shore where sun never reached and where ancient snow never melted but lay grimy and porous with age.

The yapping arctic foxes, in their shaggy summer pelts, sounded like they were coughing up cloudberry pits; the gophers whistled sharply, as though calling Nau to take notice of the shadowed mouths of their burrows, hollowed out underneath protective stones.

The seabirds shrilled from their nesting grounds atop the shoreline crags, and if they took wing all at once, disturbed by a prowling wolverine, all other sound was lost in their noisy cacophony, and the world suddenly seemed dreary, gray, and flat.

Nau was discovering that some sounds were pleasant, and there were others that made her want to run and hide. She loved to hear the birds' morning chatter above the brook; it reminded her of the whale rainbows, and the birdsong told her that something mysterious and magical was sure to come.

With each passing day the tundra was bursting into bright vivid color. Nau's feet went black from berry juice. The loyal old tundra she-wolf licked them and gazed at Nau with sadness. The she-wolf could feel the approach of winter, and of her own death. She wasn't good for much anymore; a hard life had worn down her fangs . . .

On that day, as always, Nau awoke with the sun. Its rays were bright as ever, but no longer did they hold the melting warmth of before. As they fell across her closed eyelids, she sensed a warning, an echo of impending storms.

She came fully awake then and broke her fast with a handful of cloudberries. Her keen ears pricked at the familiar murmuring of the surf, the piercing bird cries over the brook, the rustling grass.

She rose and went to the seashore.

The dew was strangely cold. Nau broke into a run, to warm herself and to shake off the last shreds of sleep. Gophers whistled after her and startled quails shot out from under her feet, but she ran on, driven by some anxious but joyful premonition. Usually she would pause at the last line of shingle by the water's edge and collect plaits of seaweed to add to her meagre breakfast, yet this time she didn't even slow.

Already she could hear the dear and familiar toot of the spouting whale cutting through the noisy surf. The gleam of sun on water blinded her, making it hard to see the shore. Then she saw something strange . . .

At first she thought it a trick of the light. The spout was there, sparkling in the sun, and so was the whale, hugging the shore. But as Nau peered at the giant of the sea, he seemed to be growing more insubstantial, as though dissolving into the cloud of water drops he had made. Nau blinked a few times, trying to clear her vision. She peered again at the whale.

There was no whale.

No spout made gleaming rainbows in the air.

Instead she saw a person standing in the foaming surf and looking back at her.

His eyes were a deep black, like a seal's. Nau looked again to the sea. There was no sign of a departing whale, only the wader birds bobbing up and down in the surf, heads twitching this way and that. Farther out, great flocks of migrating birds skimmed low over the water.

Nau stood barefoot on the icy shingle, the air around her cold. She shuddered. The man took a step toward her, and for a moment she caught a glimpse of a rainbow at his back. But now his face was changing: his eyes narrowed, his lips drew half-open, and he seemed to Nau to radiate a strange heat, a tender warmth she could feel at a distance, reaching out to her, calling her, enveloping her in a soft, balmy cloud.

She yearned to step into the stranger's embrace and warm herself there. She moved to meet him, and he took Nau by the hand.

Light and quick was his stride over the earth—stepping over puddles, leaping over streams—like the flight of a great bird. Nau followed him, her black hair streaming behind her like wings.

Now the morning's chill had vanished and the soles of Nau's feet burned as though the hot, sandy banks of tundra rivers, sun-baked in summer, carried her, and not the cool shoreline grass.

The sun chased them, lighting up the mirrorlike surface of the lagoon, skipping down the running streams and rivulets, dancing across the profusion of puddles and ponds.

But what was this?

It was joy—unfathomable and vast as the sun itself. It was a lightness of being, and a sweet, longing trepidation, a warm weight that lay upon her breast at the thought of him, the one walking beside her. The one who was all the wondrous new things of this summer—the whale giant, and the mysterious all-encompassing warmth, and the extraordinary new idea that she was different from the birds and the beasts, a thing apart from the grasses and the waves, from the sky and the earth . . .

What was happening to her?

Now they were high in the tundra hills, walking through soft, yellowing grass and on the thick layer of pale blue lichen—Arctic moss—that protected the plant roots from the harmful effects of deep permafrost. Here at the top they could see the distant sea, the pound ing of the surf reduced to a whisper.

The man paused. Nau's hand still lay in his. He turned to face the sea, and the young woman followed his gaze over the endless blue.

A whale pod frolicked just beyond the white froth of the surf. Closer and closer they came, spouting seawater into rainbows and chasing away the flocks of waders.

Once more his face shone with ardor, and a warm yellow light seemed to kindle in his great black eyes.

The man reached out for her other hand and drew her closer. The heat grew unbearable, aching and inviting all at once. Light-headed, Nau thought of the hours she had spent watching the churn of the water, the rising and falling waves, from atop the tall sea cliffs. After a while her head would spin just so, the plunging drop and endless vastness calling her, washing over her on a crest of fear and pleasure . . .

Yet this feeling was different, only a faint echo of that call from the deep. And again, this warmth—tender and soft, like the downy lining of an eider duck's nest, protection against the ever-cold cliffs it perched on, cliffs that stood ceaselessly buffeted by winds and doused in sea spray.

Up close, his face was changeable, like the light playing over the tundra and the sea, clouds drifting to reveal the sun or conceal it. He smelled of seaweed and the sea breeze. It was he and no other: he, so right and familiar, so open to her gaze, so strong and gentle. The strange unsettled mornings, the yearning dismay she'd felt watching the sun vanish over the horizon, and the delight of watching the whale nearing the beach—all these things had been premonitions of this meeting, harbingers of joy.

Sinking onto the grass, the man pulled her gently down beside him. She felt like she was unmoored inside a rainbow mist, her limbs caressed by warm jets of water, stroking her, embracing her. She was flying high over the earth, and soft, bright clouds drew her forward on a breeze, and then on, on—on a rising tide of desire to be one with him, to melt into him, desire close to agony, a pressure that filled her body and sought escape. Nau tried to hold back a cry that would not be denied, not knowing yet that this was the cry of a woman's greatest, most terrible joy, which gives birth to song, to tenderness, and to new human life.

She heard the boom of a whale spout, rending the air above the waves . . . *Rrrr-hhheu!*

"Reu, Reu, Reu," she whispered. And opened her eyes.

His face was so close that his great black eyes seemed to be drinking her in, and she felt that she was drowning in their hot, flickering depths.

Nau was not frightened anymore, nor alarmed. She was certain now that this was what she had waited for, that this was what she had lacked. Only she couldn't have known it would come to her in the form of a man who had once been a whale.

A burning pain like a sun's ray streaked through her, and she wondered how pain and joy could be as one. And answer came that there was a pain like deepest joy, a pain that made one cry out and shed bright tears of happiness. The burning ray roamed her body, igniting unseen fires, and as she drifted off, Nau found she wished it to go on endlessly.

When she came to, her first panicked thought was that it had all been a dream—but there was Reu, sitting beside her, hands full of her gleaming hair. He was smiling, and the smile filled his face with light.

He peered at Nau, touching the tip of his nose to hers, and this touch roused once more the fire that had been kindled in their hearts.

"How can such pain also be such happiness?"

"The greatest joy comes through the greatest pain," Reu answered her.

He spoke, and there again were the familiar scents from the sea—salt spray, seaweed, wet shingle, and the shattered pink starfish that dusted the beach.

At sunset, Reu rose from the grass and strode back toward the sea. Nau walked beside him. As the pounding surf grew louder in her ears, so did her dismay. This would be the first time she had approached the sea in sadness.

Here was the surf line, and the waders. Reu stopped.

The sun was falling into the water. Only a small arched sliver remained above the sea, sending a crisp, bright ribbon of light to bridge the horizon and the shingled beach. Reu stepped onto the shining path. Where a man had stood, there now rose the flicker of a whale spout.

Nau threw herself into the water, but some powerful, commanding force thrust her back onto the beach. She watched the whale go farther and farther out. His spouting jet gleamed in the very last flash of the setting sun, then vanished.

2

When the sun was high over the lagoon, Nau would go to the shore and watch for the distant rainbow that signaled the whale's approach. The sight of him, the sound of his excited, whooshing breaths, filled her with joy.

Each time, Reu would turn into a man. Hand in hand, they would walk up to where the tundra grass was soft beneath them.

They didn't speak much. A great deal of what they had to say simply flowed between them, in the way they looked at each other, in the way they touched, even in their long silences.

Days went by, their souls in invisible, inaudible flight. And then one day Nau saw that the faraway mountains were capped with snow.

"What is that?"

"That is the thing which bids me and my kin to other seas," Reu told her.

"So you are to leave me?"

Reu fell silent.

As the days grew short, so did their time together. The sun hurried to sink into the water, cutting short its journey through the sky. White snowflakes danced in the air. When the snowflakes fell onto the ground and into puddles, they turned to cold water.

The earth was growing inhospitable.

Flocks of birds set off south. The emptying tundra rang with their sad cries. Bright birdsong stilled over the once burbling spring, and its clear water went dark and dull with frequent rains.

Nau wandered the tundra looking for mouse holes to plunder, digging out the sweet roots the mice had stored away.

Some days she couldn't get near the shore at all, for giant waves crashed against the crags and threw themselves at the shingled beach, as if to grab at the lonely young woman standing on a mound of pebbles and looking out to sea. These were the days when Nau feared Reu wouldn't come again, but he always did. Still, there was a new impatience and unease in his caresses.

"Why won't you stay with me until morning?"

"Because if I don't come back to the water before the last ray of the sun is gone, I will have to stay on land forever," Reu answered her.

"But don't you want that?"

"I don't know," said Reu.

It wasn't long ago that he had frolicked, young and strong, in the spring sea, so sure that he could never trade the freedom of the water for a life on land. But now . . . how could he have known that there was a power that could turn a whale into a man, hold him to the shore, and make him forget the great danger of staying human forever?

His brothers had warned him. His father showed him the white stripe of ice along the horizon, approaching with each passing day. Soon that cold white stripe would imprison the seawater and cut off the life-giving air. Already the orcas, the whales' mortal enemies, were gone, and so were the walruses and the seals. The once teeming shallows were empty; even the smallest sea creatures had followed the larger beasts south. The shores of the northern sea grew emptier and ever more silent.

There came a day when the ice belt could be glimpsed beyond the stone promontory, radiating cold, sharp air. This time, Reu was not alone, though at first the other whales stayed back, by the edge of the ice, blowing gusts of water into the frosty fog. They were so many that even the cormorants took off in fright.

Reu approached the shore. Accompanied now by several brothers, he appeared almost to be borne aloft by them, not touching the shingle. But he fought through the foamy surf and walked out of the sea.

His chest rose and fell with each labored breath.

"Nau," he said, "I have come to you."

"Forever?"

"Forever." And as if in rejoinder, dozens of whale spouts thundered up into the sky, shattering the sunlight and drowning out all other sounds.

Reu took Nau by the hand and led her into the tundra, away from his furious kin. He walked quickly, for fear of changing his mind, of going with his whale brethren to the warm southern seas, away from the encroaching ice.

Skirting the lagoon's green shore, they walked up into the hills, where the grass was no longer so soft as before, and the earth spoke of the coming of an ancient, timeless frost—never really gone, but only hiding from the summer sun beneath a thick layer of moss and old grasses.

They settled on a knoll and sat together for a long time, silent. Sadness clouded Reu's face like an autumn fog, and Nau touched a finger to his cheek. He startled, then sighed.

"What will we do?" asked Nau.

"We will live," he told her curtly. "A new kind of life. A human life."

Hard they were, those first days of winter. Reu dug out an earthen shelter, propping its walls up with tree branches scavenged from the shore and roofing it over with a layer of sod and dried grass. He made a pike from a broken walrus bone and killed a wild deer, and Reu and Nau laid the deerskin atop their bed, to stave off the ancient cold of the earth.

Their carefree summer days now seemed to her a bright dream, unreal. Sometimes, looking at the endless white desert of the sea, riven with gigantic ice hummocks and shards, shining with a cold glow, Nau couldn't believe that Reu had ever been a whale at all. The wind riffled through the piles of upended ice floes, then clambered onto the shore, shrouding everything along its path in snow. It raged above the low earthen cave, trying to level it with the snow-covered plain. And it raged and howled all the more when each morning it discovered a freshly melted black opening steaming with human, living breath.

Each nightfall found the first people of the narrow spit between the lagoon and the sea nearly toppling with exhaustion—but they were happy. The immense, unbreakable bond that had first joined Nau and Reu still flamed between them with all the steady power of the long summer sun.

Reu had much luck with hunting, and soon they had enough deerskin to gird themselves against the cold.

Nau fashioned thread from dried deer tendons, and, with an orca-bone needle, sewed the cured skins together. Spreading the skins fur side down on the floor of their cramped earthen hut, she used her strong, rough heels to pound them into softness, so that Reu might be more comfortable wearing them close to his body.

The darkness came closer and more impenetrable each day. All they saw of the sun was a narrow red ribbon. But the fire from their stone lamp burned like a little sun, a visitor to their heavily snow-dowsed home. And both Reu and Nau believed that each new day would be beautiful—as beautiful as each of them was to the other, each morning they woke to each other. For them, it was as though the past did not exist. The most important things—the life-giving warmth of their home, the light of the lamp—were in the here and now. These things were real. Tomorrow depended on today.

Storms blew often. Walls of wet, compacted snow and strong wind could funnel up into the air and knock them off their feet, press them into the ground.

Once, listening to the clanging snow on the roof, Nau felt a sudden kick—from the inside.

"What is in there?" She pressed her hand to her belly, alarmed.

Reu laid his hand on the warm, swarthy skin just above his wife's belly button. He felt life stir within.

"It is new life!" Reu's voice rang with joy. "It is another bright morning of our lives. The reason we are together!"

"A new life," Nau said softly, listening to her body.

When the snowstorm passed, Nau and Reu stepped out from their home and saw the sun peeking above the far-off mountains. "It's come back! The source of all warmth!" they cried out in delight, gazing happily at each other.

The sun was low yet, and its rays colored the snow crimson all the way to the barely discernible horizon.

Reu busied himself making tools. Watching him, the way the hair fell on his face, Nau had a vague memory of something extraordinary, some strange and magical thing that had happened to her long ago. Had it been a dream? Could Reu really have been a whale?

Every day, at dawn, Reu would set off for the pack ice. Nau waited for him, anxiously scanning the shore. Sometimes she thought she could see open water far out to sea, green waves alight with faraway rainbows. What were they? Her heart would race, and flushed with a rising heat, she'd have to push back her deerskin hood.

But upon Reu's return, Nau forgot all about her strange thoughts and imaginings, too busy with butchering the kill and preparing their meal.

~ℓ~

The sun broke away from the top of the Far-off Crags and sailed across the sky. Reu, peering at the south face of a large ice hummock, could see a stubble of tiny icicles.

One morning, Nau was awakened by familiar birdsong, so close that she wondered at first whether the bird was indoors with her. Nau peered outside. It was a little gray snow bunting, hopping about on thin, shivery legs and twittering brightly as she pecked at crumbs of food. As she sang, she kept her sly black eye on Nau, as if congratulating her on the return of the Great Light.

As the shallows became warmer, the fat seals returned to shore. They clambered out to bask in the sun, and the hunter was ready for them. Some days he brought home several seals and was then able to spend the next few days fixing up their wind-battered home, instead of going to hunt.

The first people would stand on the sunny side of the lagoon, where the snow had already melted, talking of the future. Nau had grown round and heavy. She struggled to carry her big belly around.

"Time will pass," Reu would say to her thoughtfully, "and there will be other homes, next to ours, and the people of the family we have started will spread out across the seashore. There is plenty of space, plenty of beasts in the sea and herds of deer in the tundra—everything needful for life and the promise of the future . . ."

"I like thinking about the future," Nau would reply. "Looking ahead you get a dizzy sort of feeling, like looking down from a great height."

Snow was melting all around the lagoon, its frozen surface now pocked and pitted like a moldy deerskin.

One day Reu ran down from the heights, where he had been looking out for migrating deer, with exciting news: "I saw open water."

Nau felt alarmed by this. "Open water?" she echoed.

"The ice has broken," Reu told her. "Great flocks of birds are flying down to the water. Soon they'll be overhead."

"Where do they come from, all these creatures that keep coming here?"

"There must be another land somewhere," said Reu. "Maybe more people, like you and me. It's just that we haven't met them yet."

Another day they awoke to the sound of warm, pattering rain. Venturing out, they saw that the lagoon was free of ice, except for a few large pieces being carried out to sea by the tide. Behind them, too, on the other side of the spit, they could now glimpse open water. The breeze carried with it the half-forgotten scent of the sea, full of mysterious promise.

Reu wove a net from deer tendons and stretched it over a

hoop made from a pliant branch. He went climbing up on the shoreline crags and caught scores of red-beaked tufted puffins. The last of the ice floes departed from the lagoon. Nau felt a strange and uncontrollable pull toward the water. She could have spent every day just sitting on the shore, watching the smooth surface of the sea, the plump cormorants diving for fish, the darting gray gobies and the flatfish keeping low to the underwater shingle.

It happened early one morning, when the sun was high over the nearest cape and about to set off on a long journey above the tundra hills. Nau made her way down to a small clearing near the water, where a swift stream ran to the sea through fresh, shining grass. At her cries, Reu hurried to her side.

"Help me into the water," Nau pleaded.

The whale calves arrived just as the seawater touched her legs. Straightaway the newborns were swimming and spouting. Nau turned to Reu blissfully.

"I am glad that they are like you."

She walked into the water, her swollen breasts pillowed on the waves. The calves drew close and began to suckle noisily, tickling her with their soft, thick lips, pinkly glistening with the first furry traces of whalebone.

Every day Reu went to hunt the earless seals that we now call *nerpa*, or ringed seal, and the larger, bearded seals, *lakhtak*, out on the treacherous ice field still stuck fast and ringing the shore. Nau, however, rarely left the shore of the lagoon; she was busy looking after her babies, who were growing bigger and stronger by the hour and soon became bold enough to venture into the deepest part of the lagoon. This alarmed her, and she would call them back by their father's name: "Reu! Reu! Reu!"

The calves would spout in reply and rush back to nuzzle her breasts with their soft mouths, relishing the fatty milk and drinking their fill.

When, at the close of day, the sun sank into the water—as if to wash away the aches of a long, arduous trip over the earth—the children's father would always come to play with them. He tossed colorful stones far into the water, and the calves frolicked, retrieving them from the bottom of the lagoon.

Then the lagoon grew noisy with the brisk splashing of the baby whales and the hiss and whistle of their jetting spouts, and with their parents' delighted cries. The sounds mingled with birdsong over the brook and the flapping of seagull wings as they hurriedly got out of the little whales' way. Gophers watched from hillocks, whistling approvingly.

At sunset it was time for the calves to retreat deeper into the water to sleep; on the beach, their parents bedded down on some deerskins. Nau would wake in the night and, holding her breath, listen for her children's sleepy exhalations amid the splash and surf. She would lie awake and stare into the pallid sky, starless for now; the stars would appear as the days grew shorter. She was one with the breeze gently fluttering over the somnolent grasses and flowers, and the waves slapping at the beach. She was part of the stony shore, washed by icy oceanic waters, and the clouds underneath the pale, sharp-edged moon. She was everything at once, all the wide world that lay around her, filling every visible void. She knew that it would all end with the coming of the dawn. When the first rays of sunlight broke on the wet stone crags, leapt onto the shingled beach, and sparkled on the lagoon waters, she would once more be a creature separate from the natural world, circumscribed. It was always in daylight that Nau brooded on her children, who, though they were one flesh with her and Reu, were nevertheless whales and not people, and could not gain the shore, nor enter the home of their parents. She consoled herself with the faint hope that one day the calves would turn into people, as their father had done.

Nau sometimes wished that she could share these troubling thoughts with Reu, but he seemed not to notice any difference between himself and the baby whales. Perhaps it was that he still thought of himself as a whale.

In daylight Nau had to puzzle hard to know what the old raven, sitting atop the ancient walrus skull, bleached and polished to a shine, wanted from her. She didn't immediately understand the songs of the snow buntings or the whistling of gophers. And this alarmed her, and made her wonder what was happening to her.

Reu, meanwhile, was occupied from sunrise until sunset. Back in the spring, he had harpooned several walruses out on the ice and had shown Nau how to split the skins so they stretched supple and thin. He let the skins soak in the lagoon for a long time, while he gathered together thin sheaves of floating driftwood. It looked like he was constructing the skeleton of some strange, vast fish. He whittled down each plank with a stone blade and polished them smooth; then bored holes in them, using tubular animal bones; and finally lashed them together with sealskin thongs. When the structure was complete, Reu retrieved the walrus hides from the water and stretched them over the wooden frame.

"This boat," he explained to Nau, "will let us go far into the water."

The trial cruise took place in the lagoon. Fast-flowing water beat a cheerful tattoo against the boat's taut, leathery hide, and the sealskin sail filled with wind. The boat all but flew across the lagoon. The whale babies followed behind, joyfully skimming across the water and trying to splash their parents with their spouts.

The boat sailed along the shingled bar, heading for the strait that linked the lagoon with open water. Nau shouted endearments to her children and imagined that they called back to her in youthful voices, admiring their father's invention. Reu was shouting, too, proud of his miraculous creation, and his voice rang out, forceful and stirring. Fat cormorants gave way unwillingly, beating their wings slowly to lift from the water; seagulls dashed shrieking overhead; and nerpa, bobbing up on the waves, gazed intently in the family's wake, exceedingly puzzled by the proceedings and wondering what manner of strange beast had come among them.

When at last they returned to shore, Nau turned to Reu happily: "Now we are closer to our children."

"Tomorrow, the open sea," Reu told her.

And the sea received them gently. Nau felt its vast, mighty power and marveled at the high waves that had been invisible from shore. How easily they carried the hide boat aloft! A strong, steady wind drew them farther and farther away from land.

Reu's face glowed with some emotion Nau had never seen before. He seemed to be one with the boat, indivisible. Each breaking wave and gust of wind found an answering echo in him; each time the boat reached a crest, Reu let out a strange, short breath, just like a spouting whale might. The wind played in his hair and caressed his tense, clenched features, drawing tears from his wide-open eyes.

And then Reu began to shout, loudly and plangently— wondrous, rainbow-bright words:

> *O wind, gusty wind,*
> *That mingles with fine sea spray!*
> *Take up my hide boat*
> *On your mighty shoulders, and lift me*
> *To the paths of my seagoing kin*
> *So I may meet them once more, and tell them*
> *Of the great power that lives in nature*
> *And can turn whale into man, and give life*
> *To new things, which were once unknown . . .*

Borne along by the hypnotic rhythm of Reu's chant, Nau, too, was shouting into the wind. The newly born song—the first human song—mingled with the wind and rang out against the sail.

The shingled bar had long since faded from view, and the multihued ferns and lichens that riddled the stony coastline could not be distinguished. In the distance, the crags looked blue and smudged, and small. The great swath of water dividing boat from shore filled Reu with excitement and gave him new strength.

But after a time Nau grew frightened. Safe, known earth was now far behind them. She couldn't make out their little home.

"Where are we going, Reu?"

Reu broke off his song, and the last of the sound rose up over the sail and dissipated among the hiss and tumult of the waves. A dark cloud seemed to pass across his face, and his exultation vanished.

Quietly, he answered: "I don't know." He sat down on the lashed wooden ribs of the boat. "I was thinking of the past," he told her. "I was young then, and curious. I often swam apart from the others, and went far into the open water; I loved to feel as one with the sea, the wind, and the blue sky. I was warned, but I didn't listen to my elders. Once, a pod of killer whales came after me. They hunted and harried me fiercely, driving me closer and closer to the shore. It was a long chase, but I managed to evade them and reunite with my pod. Another time, I was trapped among great shards of floating ice, and barely managed to make it out, scraped and bleeding. Today, out on the open sea, I felt young and full of life again."

Reu turned the boat homeward.

As they approached the lagoon, a whale spout suddenly soared from the water, and there was the head of a whale, right beside the boat.

"It's one of my brothers!" Reu was delighted. "And look, Nau, there's another! And one behind us! They came to meet me! Nau, they are happy to see us!"

The whales approached the fragile vessel with care and nudged it helpfully toward the beach. Their wide-open mouths, fenced with whalebone, seemed to Nau to be smiling.

Reu had risen to his feet. He was beaming to see his brothers.

"What a shame they don't understand human language," Nau said.

"They understand it well enough," Reu told her, "but speaking it is another matter. To speak, you must become a human, fall in love with a woman like I did. . . . That's what my mother told me when she found out why I was drawn to the beach, why I was so long gone from the pod each day. And she told me, too, that all the humans who live by the shore are descended from whales transformed by love."

"So we are not alone?"

"Maybe not," said Reu.

"Why, then, did I give birth to whales?"

"Because I am a whale," said Reu. And just at that moment, like an echo of his words, the whales all leapt powerfully up and nearly out of the water, their vast, long bodies shining. The waves they raised nearly swamped the boat, but Reu only laughed and shouted joyfully to his brothers.

Nau shared his pleasure. The nearer they came to the shore and the line of the surf, the less anxious she felt.

Reu aimed the boat for the entrance to the lagoon. There, their children met them, swimming alongside the boat.

Toward sunset, Nau fed the children, and they swam off to the middle of the lagoon.

As the humans ate their evening repast, Reu said, "My brothers acknowledged me. They saw I had come back, that I still belonged to the sea."

എ

When the morning dew turned frosty and the tundra berries were at their juiciest, Nau began to notice that her children were struggling to swim close to her. They had grown up.

Rising with the sun, Nau would walk up into the green hills to fill her hide satchel with black crowberries, wild blueberries, and ripe, crimson cloudberries, returning to their hut in the noonday sun. Reu would still be out; each morning he sailed to the Far-off Crags, which thrust up sharply from the sea, where he hunted nerpa, harpooned walrus, and met with his brothers.

Nau would mix up the berries with a quantity of nerpa fat and set them outside to freeze, a delicious treat for the hunter's return.

Later, she would stand on the shingled spit, facing seaward, awaiting the sight of Reu's boat. First the sail would appear. It would grow taller, swaying slightly in the breeze. Birds flew overhead, pointing the way home, and alongside, the whale-brothers cruised.

Nau would watch the boat come in until she could make out the face of the hunter, his black hair streaming in the wind, and the nerpa and walrus carcasses lashed to the sides of the boat.

Today, Reu was dragging in a huge walrus; its yellow tusks poked out of the water. The two of them struggled to get the huge beast onto the shore.

"This walrus has a great big hide," said Reu. "We will stretch it over a new hut, a more spacious one."

He had long known that Nau would be a mother again and was pleased to see her time approaching.

As winter neared and nights grew darker, the baby whales stopped coming close to shore; they had grown too big to swim into the shallows. Nau no longer breastfed them, and they had learned to feed themselves.

"The lagoon is too cramped for them," said Reu, as he readied the boat one day. As Nau settled in the bottom, he took the prow, the better to adjust the sail and steer.

The whales awaited their parents in the deepest part of the

lagoon. Reu called out, "Follow me! Follow our boat!" And so the children fell in beside the stern. They were always happy to see their father and mother. Reu steered for the strait.

Nau was silent as she gazed at the little whales. Whenever they raised their heads from the water, their bright, clear eyes shone with unspoken tenderness and filial loyalty. It was a sight that warmed her to the core and made her wish she could join them in the water, swimming alongside them down the wide, shimmering path to the open sea.

On reaching the bay, the little whales paused, as though saying farewell to the lagoon that had cradled them. Before them lay the open sea—wide, mighty, and deep, full of new discoveries, new friends, and kin.

Nau looked ahead and saw Reu's brothers waiting. No sooner had the children left the lagoon than they were ringed by adult whales, spouting and trumpeting their joy.

"Now they will be safe," said Reu. "They are where they ought to be, in deep water and among their whale kin."

Nau gazed at her departing children with sadness.

"Do not grieve," Reu told her, laying a comforting hand upon her shoulder. "We will have more children . . . though all children, when they grow up, leave their home for a new life that belongs only to them."

The children returned to the lagoon many times. They did everything to show Nau and Reu how hale and happy they were, and how well they remembered their parents.

When the ribbon of encroaching ice first showed on the horizon, Nau gave birth to twin boys. They lay on either side of their happy mother and screamed fit to burst. When Reu bent over them for a closer look, his expression was hard to read. Was he pleased with them or not?

Their older siblings had gone to warmer waters only the day before, to winter there, safe from sharp ice floes and deadly frosts. The entire pod had come to bid Nau and Reu goodbye, playing close to shore for a long while, and alarming the flocks of migrating birds.

The beach grew bare and empty. The ice sheet, creaking malevolently and rustling as it crept past the shallows, ranged nearer each day. The wind raged ever harder, lashing the shingled beach with the kind of sleet that could turn into snow before one's very eyes.

Inside the hut, the two baby boys kept up a din that carried far and wide, threading human voices into the howl of the winds.

As she held them close, Nau thought of her first, silent babies who had been born whales and who had left for the far seas. How wonderful it was to be a mother!

‎﷽‎

Reu was busy building a large new *yaranga*.

First, he erected a semicircle of tall poles and covered them over with untreated walrus hide. Then he constructed a conical top and covered this, too, with hides that were fresh, so that daylight, falling through them, seemed yellower and warmer. For real warmth, though, they would need a *polog*—a heavy, shielding curtain—which Nau sewed from a polar bear skin.

There were baskets of hardened hide and wooden barrels brimming with walrus fat, and the earthen pit outside stored plenty of frozen meat. The people of the shore awaited the coming winter without fear, for now they were not alone among the snows, facing the icebound Sea of Whales.

Every spring the whales returned. Nau brought her boys to the shore and pointed out the whales, saying, "Look, there are your brothers!"

The brother-whales swam close to shore, their great heads nearly touching the shingle. They dipped their heads under, then surfaced suddenly and showered Nau and the boys with warm water.

The boys dashed to and fro, shouting and excited. Their mother often had to drag them out of the surf.

They'd all come home wet from head to toe. Nau was forever drying out and mending the boys' clothes and sewing new *torbasses* and *kukhliankas*. They seemed to grow out of everything with manic speed.

The whales accompanied Reu on his hunts and often helped out when his boat was heavily laden and slow in the water.

> *Whales and humans are one people!*
> *Joining together, the land and the sea*
> *Gave birth to a nation whose pastures*
> *Lie in the waves and in the deep waters*
> *And, in winter, among the ice hummocks!*

The boys heard their father's mighty voice carried from the sea and listened with wonder to his song.

> *The waves of the sea, growing still,*
> *Became the hills of the tundra,*
> *Overgrew with grass, gone speckled with berries;*

And all that lives upon the tundra
Has kin in the waves upon the sea . . .

The boys would go to the surf and join their father in the refrain:

Whales and humans are one nation!
We are the kin that spans sea and land!
We are born in eternal friendship!

The humans dragged their kill out on the beach to butcher it, to the delighted shrieks of seagulls whizzing over the chunks of meat and blubber. The waves lapped gently at the draining blood, and whale spouts shone far out on the sea, bisecting the sky and fracturing the sun's rays into glittering curtains.

Winters and summers came, one after the other. The first-born human sons grew bigger; other children came in their wake. But there were no more whales born to the first people of the Shingled Spit.

Early in spring, as soon as the sharp southerly wind tore the ice away from the shoreline, someone would be the first to spot the whale spout appearing on the horizon and would greet the returning kin:

"Our brothers are coming! Our brothers are swimming to meet us!"

As Nau and Reu grew old, the people they had made and raised—not only men, but women—grew up. New yarangas were pitched next to the first, new hearths came alight, and virginal hearthstones grew thick with soot.

Reu was too old for hunting now, and his sons—strong and fearless men—took his place. These men had needed names, for they resembled one another just as their giant seagoing ancestors did. The two eldest were called Tynen, which means "Sunrise," and Tyneviri, "One Who Came Down with the Dawn." The other sons, too, were named according to their personalities or events that took place at their births. One was named Vukvun—"Stone"—and another Keral'gin, after the northeast wind that blew especially fiercely on the morning of his birth. The girls also had names. There was Tynena—"Little Sunrise"—and Tytyna—"Twilight."

But autumn comes to human lives just as it does to the natural world. One day Reu asked Nau to make him a pair of white *camuss* trousers, using hide from the legs of a mature buck. This meant that the old man was preparing to go through the clouds and leave the earthbound world.

One stormy evening, as rain lashed at the wet roofs of their dwellings and wind ran along the walls, seeking an opening, Reu gathered together all of his descendants.

"Soon I will leave you," he told them tranquilly, resting his gaze for a moment upon each and every assembled face. "As soon as the clouds lift and the way up into the sky is clear, I will begin my long journey. . . . But before I depart, I wish to speak with you all. The most important wisdom I leave you with is to never forget you have mighty kindred. You are descended from the giants of the sea, and every whale is your brother. To be a brother does not require that you look the same. Kinship means much more than that. When you climb to the highest crags and peer down, how often do you see tall rocks that look like people? Yet it would not occur to you to call them brothers, or to think you have come from cold stone. . . . We came to live upon the earth because of the greatest expression that life can have: the Great Love. It made us into humans, made me into a human. And as long as you love one another, love your brothers, you will remain human beings. Love is all-present. I think that we cannot be alone in this world. The old tales of my whale kin tell of others like me, so there may well be other Shingled Spits out there, where yarangas ring the shore and your human brothers hunt nerpa and walrus, singing songs of the sea. Find your brothers, and multiply, for only in unity will you be strong. And remember one more thing: my journey beyond the clouds lies through the sea . . ."

There was an astonishing congregation of whales by the Shingled Spit that year, as though they had all come to say farewell to their brother. One by one they approached the shore. Reu sat silently, facing the water. Sometimes Nau came to sit beside him, and they spoke of their youth, when Great Love came to the lonely beach to unite a whale and a human.

Reu's thoughts turned to those he was leaving behind, in the sea and on land. He was satisfied with his fate. Probably he was happy. He had been the one to become a human, to know firsthand the Great Love of the ancient whale lore. Now everyone thought that what had happened to Reu was the stuff of legends. . . . Surely, then, a legend could be said to be a truth that people had ceased to believe in.

How wonderful it had been to live beside Nau! He had found a world entire, with all its beauty and tenderness, in this one woman, whose heart was wider than the sky and whose warmth matched that of the sun. It was her Great Love that had made Reu into a man. Reu turned to look at her. The long years had brushed Nau's black hair with snow, and her face with wrinkles. Even so, she was herself and beautiful.

Gazing at her face, Reu felt his heart swell with tenderness and gratitude. For now, she would stay with their children. And when the time came, she would join him in eternity.

"I was happy with you," Reu told her.

ؘ࣭࣪

He died as the winter ice came to shackle the sea and the first powdery snow fell over the cracks and melt-holes. His sons carried out the ritual of farewell.

They dressed Reu in white funerary garments and tied his fur-lined *malakhai* hat firmly around his head. By his yaranga's entrance, they lit a fire and passed the body over its cleansing flames. After placing Reu atop a sledge, the men stepped into their harnesses and went toward the sea, the runners creaking sharply as they ran over the fresh snow.

Nau, wearing a dark-colored *kerk'her*, watched her husband depart for eternity. She grieved but did not wail. Reu had come to the end of his earth journey and had left them with the dignity befitting a man who had completed all his duties.

It was a still, clear day. A cold sun shed miserly light onto the cortege dragging the funeral sledge over the ice hummocks toward the flat, white expanse beyond. A large ice hole was already prepared.

Nau never looked away, but now a tear rolled unbidden down her cheek, leaving a cold trail and dropping, like a shard of salty sea ice, onto her lips. How big and sad this world was! How hard it was to measure the span of your life all the way from the distant past, barely remembered, to the mist-shrouded future in the undiscovered country of the sky, where there is no death nor knowledge of another world . . . and everything along this journey was the stuff of life itself, a life that would carry on beyond the clouds with more force and duration than earth-bound existence. . . . How big and sad this world was!

Their sons pulled the sledge in silence, picking out the smoothest route through the ice hummocks, so as not to disturb the body that would now sleep forever.

The water on the ice hole's inner edges rose and fell, as though the sea itself, the cradle of Reu's first breaths, sighed in sorrow. The surface soon churned with slush. With a ladle made of stiff deer antler and bound with lakhtak-hide thongs, one of Reu's sons cleared the ice away again, revealing the dark green, almost black, water beneath. He looked toward his brothers.

Wordlessly, they unstrapped their father's body from the sledge and laid it onto the ice, feet toward the water. After a moment's pause, they gave the body a push, and it slid into the water with a surprising quickness and grace.

The sledge followed, sinking immediately to the bottom, as though it were made of heavy walrus bone and not light wood.

The eldest of the brothers peered into the water and saw the reflected sky and Reu's receding face. Their father was smiling, saying farewell to the sons he was leaving behind.

And in the sky above, the sun sat low and shone on the horizon. The world was silent, as though all living things stood in awed prayer before the wonder of Great Love.

Part II

1

Enu sat by the fire, listening attentively as Nau spoke. For some time now, many of the inhabitants of the Shingled Spit had brushed aside her stories as only the ramblings of an old woman. She was something of a local sight, and travelers sharing news from other places would usually find time to inquire after the old lady's health, and to hear her tales and teachings.

Enu did not let on that he didn't really believe old Nau. Anyway, who knew? Perhaps she was right—never mind that her tales were all outrageously unlikely, especially the one about her youth as the wife of a whale, and her whale children. No one could guess at her true age. Even the eldest of the old men swore that she was already ancient when they were just young boys, and even then full of the same tiresome stories about people tracing their descent to whales.

Enu studied Nau's lined face, all wrinkled like a baked walrus skin, and each time he really looked into her deep, remarkable eyes, glimmering green like the ocean, he found himself uneasy.

Nau had no home of her own. She could step inside any yaranga on the Shingled Spit, make herself comfortable, and remain there for days, sometimes months. She insisted that all the people were her descendants, and maybe it truly was so. No one would have thought of refusing her shelter or food. And yet, when she moved on to another yaranga, her hosts would breathe a sigh of relief. No one asked her to stay longer.

Despite his youth, Enu was held to be the wisest man in the village. He knew everything that a skilled healer, seer of weather, and keeper of ancient customs must know. But there was one thing that Enu could not say with certainty, and that was whether old Nau spoke the truth about the origins of the coastal peoples. It was true that the people of the Shingled Spit esteemed the sea giants just as they might their ancestors, and yet how different were the men of the land and the whales of the water. Whales were so much bigger, and silent—they had no voices of their own. An inconvenient kind of ancestor, one whom it was hard to know how to honor. Still, no one would ever say so to her face, since the cult of the whale ancestors had now been observed for many generations.

Old Nau watched the fire impassively, and Enu could see the firelight smothered in the endless dark depths of her eyes.

"It was through me," she said in a low voice, "that the land and the sea joined together, through my body that human beings were born the way we see them today."

"What about words?" Enu asked tentatively. "Thoughts?"

"When I was young, I dashed about the springy tundra hillocks, cold and soft with groundwater, like a doe. I had no inkling of what I was—a sable, a wolf, a wolverine—and it made no difference to me. Not until Reu came and gave me the gift of Great Love. And Great Love was a mystery, too, because we knew not whence it had sprung, to come to us. This mystery gave birth to thought; while there is mystery, humans will always try to use reason to solve it." She fell silent.

"So what you're saying is that while there's mystery, there will be reason," Enu said courteously.

"That's right," Nau told him.

"Where does speech come from, then?" Enu was genuinely intrigued. "How did people learn to speak and communicate with one another?"

"Reu and I wanted badly to speak to each other. And so we found the words."

Enu furrowed his brow. It was all too simple somehow . . .

"Things, you understand, have a life of their own, regardless of people naming and measuring them," Nau continued. "But of all the living creatures, only humans have words. And speech is what makes us human."

Enu now found he was listening not just with his mind but with his heart. Truly there was something of great meaning and wisdom in her words. For the old lady, the world had always been whole, unified, and complete, and the whale had always been the part of it she most revered.

"So where did the other gods, like the four winds, come from?" Enu attempted to tread carefully.

"There aren't any gods," Nau snapped. "People just made them up, because they feared mystery. When you can't be bothered to use reason to understand mystery, that's when you make up gods. As many gods as there are mysteries in the world. You can blame everything on gods. Whenever a person shows weakness, some strange powers must be involved. These days people even say their own powers are gods-given. Disgraceful!"

"We do revere the whales, though," Enu pointed out.

"A whale is not a god," Nau said with some force. "He is simply our ancestor and our brother. He lives beside us, always ready to come to our aid. That's all there is to it."

ملا

Enu brooded on this as he tramped along the beach, bending down to pinch off bits of seagrass and popping them absent-mindedly into his mouth. The damp wind, reeking of seaweed, birds, fishes, and animals, distracted him and scattered his thoughts. Instinctively he felt the merciless and terrifying truth of what Nau had said: that men had made a multitude of gods from their great fear of the unknown. It was an unnerving thought, but also appealing in its simplicity. What, then, should they do about their own long-settled customs? It would be hard to give up the familiar, harder still to give up gods. . . . Common sense told him it would be a mistake to try to upend people's beliefs entirely, even if they were false.

And what to make of old Nau herself? Her very name was the stuff of legend, her story overgrown with mystery. She had said that mysteries spurred the human mind to doing and discovering. She was right in that. And yet reason itself seemed always at the ready to accept an easy solution to the riddle, or a weak semblance of the truth, full of holes and inconsistencies.

How long had Nau walked the earth? She had often said that in the beginning she was all alone and did not know herself from a sable or a wolverine, or a gopher. Could it be that she really had been some kind of animal, all the way back?

But as for her mating with a whale . . . a whale who through the power of Great Love had become a *man* . . .

There were many stories of whales helping the coastal people hunt and keeping them from harm in the water. No one disbelieved these fables, exactly. But this business of a whale changing into a human . . . why had that never happened again? Everyone knew about *ter'yky*, the changeling creatures who had once been hunters, borne away on an ice floe and then returning to haunt the village. Out on the cold sea, the creature's clothes would shred and tear away, yet he would not die. Such a man might grow coarse hair all over his body, like a lakhtak's fur, his features growing seallike, too, his speech deserting him.

Such changelings had been seen in the tundra, wandering near human villages. They stole food, breaking into cold storage pits and tugging drying meat from hanging lines. They were known to attack women—and then there would be babies born with hairy heads and faces, sometimes dumb and deaf, or unseeing.

Ter'yky, yes. But after the humans fathered by Reu, no other people had ever been transformed from a whale again.

Still, how to explain the reverence their people had for whales, from the ancient days to now, and the tender regard in which these giant beasts were held by all? And on the other hand—how could one fail to respect and revere these creatures, whose gigantic bodies raised the highest waves, and whose great exhalations reached up into the sky? All other sea life stayed well clear of men, fearing them; whales alone sought encounter, always meeting the hide boats when they went out to sea. More than once, Enu himself had seen whales leading hunters to the hidden places where seals and walruses swarmed.

Enu knew that his people did not really believe old Nau's stories. They were only tales for children, dreamed up by a senile old woman. And yet there was a silent, common understanding that to voice any doubt in Nau's presence would be sacrilege.

Though she never set herself up as a healer or fortune-teller, old Nau never refused anyone who came to her for help. Her remedies were mainly herbal, tinctures of plants and roots. Her predictions were so precise as to frighten people—perhaps because she foretold both troubles and joys with the same remote indifference—and because she never concealed the truth, not many dared her advice. On the contrary, most villagers, wary of her sharp tongue, actively avoided speaking about matters of import with Nau around. They relied instead on Enu, who knew how to soften bad news with consolingly vague predictions and promises.

How long had Nau walked the earth? Could she really be as eternal as the seaward crags, the hills and rocky coastlines of their land? Yet she was aging, too; she was deeply marked by time and living.... How immeasurably ancient she must be, she who claimed to remember the first humans, even now, when the shores and the tundra teemed with people.

Everyone was used to seeing the deer herds grazing, staying perfectly calm at the herders' approach. You could even use them to pull a sledge, like dogs. And yet Nau told stories of how, when Reu was still alive, the deer were wild, and the first people had to sneak up on them if they wanted to catch one. No sledge dogs either, just large wolves who prowled the tundra, coming close only to steal meat from the storage pits, though on a quiet moonlit night you could hear them howling fit to chill the blood.

The old songs called this the Sea of Whales—the great and mysterious body of water that lapped gently at his feet as he walked. How strange and different was life within the deep, with only its faint echoes washing up on shore: loopy jellyfish, prickly red starfish, seashells, little shrimps and mollusks.

Yet how strange, too, the world of stars and sky! You needed only to look up overhead, into that dark void that yet blazed with celestial fires, to feel your heart and soul trembling with a holy terror. The bright ring of the moon might reflect a human face, or the shades of dead kin, or the figures of living people who hunt and eat just as the inhabitants of the earth do. How, then, could anyone deny the possibility of many worlds, or of the mysterious, mighty powers pervading and connecting these worlds, the outer forces that were named *K'elet*, "gods"?

All right, let the whales be revered as ancestors—but it would be a mistake to neglect these other gods.

Not everyone was able to perceive the great powers at work, to know many things. Fate chose a few from the many and gave them not merely sight of the future and knowledge of the surrounding world but insight into things beyond human ken. These were powers given to them for the good of all people, to use in their service.

So where did Nau fit in?

It was a good and honorable thing to be descendants of whales. Awareness of this special ancestry lifted people up and made them strive to be as strong and independent as the sea giants themselves. And yet these origins were also cloaked in mystery—a mystery that could be truly understood only by someone deserving, chosen by destiny. If that were true, then Nau was the person who had most earned their reverence.

But Nau, of course, put people off. On and on she went, with prosaic details that could only weaken her listeners' faith in their whale beginnings: for example, how Reu, their progenitor, used to snore at night. She insisted that the most ludicrous part of her stories—like giving birth to whale babies, meaning every nearby whale was also her direct descendant—was literally true. Why talk this way, when it only irritated people?

Perhaps the kinship of humans and whales had a kind of mythical truth. But myths were meant to be majestic, noble, inaccessible to the common man: a mysterious origin story that shone from a distance, like the snowcapped faraway mountains, not one debased by mundane details.

And what to do about Nau herself? She looked as though she wouldn't last much longer. She was terribly old, though, surprisingly, she never complained of anything, never coughed and wheezed like the other elderly women. Could she really be immortal?

Enu stopped and looked back down the beach.

He saw a small, bent figure, easily recognisable as Nau, standing near the shore. Just beyond the foamy swells of the surf, two whales greeted her, heads high above the water, sending up fizzing, iridescent jets.

2

The hunters, in their boat, were heading far out to sea. A sprightly wind rang like a bell through their sail, fashioned from thin nerpa hides, expertly tanned and well bleached in sharp human piss. The men scanned the sea intently, looking for the round heads of bobbing lakhtak and nerpa, or the whiskery faces of walruses.

Two harpooners sat ready at the stern, balancing their long spears, sharply tipped with obsidian, across their laps. These tips were cleverly designed: they came away when the spear lodged in an animal's hide, twisting sideways and becoming harder to shake off, while still linked to the spear by a hide thong, like a leash.

Enu occupied the bow, clad in a waterproof coat of walrus intestines—a yellowish, rustling material that guarded against the salty sea damp, protecting his inner garments of soft, fuzzy skins taken from the young deer of early spring. With one hand on the tiller and the other holding the end of the line, he was able to pilot the boat and maintain a good speed even when counter to the wind.

This was a busy season for the birds that lived on the sea; the flocks, having fattened up and raised a new generation of young, were gathering to begin their autumn migration to parts unknown.

Enu supposed that the birds would go to a place where the summer never ended, where there were no winter frosts and the sea, in all likelihood, did not freeze either. If you watched the birds in flight, and studied the path of the whales, it was obvious that they all went toward the noonday sun, exactly the spot where the red skies of deep winter betokened an invisible dawn. Only a few remained behind to wait out the long cold season.

What kind of place, wondered Enu, has seas that don't freeze in winter? And then it came to him with a jolt: when the sun came back to his home, it must leave the other places behind, and then it would be their turn for winter!

He was about to share his revelation with his boatmates, when he thought better of it and held his peace. Why tell them? They wouldn't understand it, not really. They wouldn't understand that if you followed the sun, forward and back again, you could live in an endless summer, just as the whales did. . . . Enu was sweating with excitement. So this was the secret to happiness, this unending journey toward warmth. In these parts, a person's main concern was evading the lethal breath of the cold. As soon as summer arrived, the women would drag their winter pologs outside to begin the annual mending, patching worn-out places with new pieces of polar bear fur. And toward autumn, they'd gather up dried grass to pack around the polog, to help keep warmth indoors. Most important, though, was the fire that lived in the stone blubber lamps, which had to be constantly looked after. Warmth was life itself; anyone who could find a way to perpetual warmth would be a genuine savior of his people.

Deep in rumination, Enu had lost all interest in the progress of the hunt. How marvelous was the working of reason: no sooner had you come onto one interesting thought than another, and then another, unspooled in its wake. If you considered the very long winter season and short summer hereabouts, then you realized the sun must spend a much longer time elsewhere . . . which meant that in the land of the noonday sun, summers were long and winters short. If only they could find the way there, the land of the long warmth!

Enu startled and came to, clutching the tiller in a perspiring grip. It took him a moment to understand what the harpooners were shouting: they'd spotted a herd of walruses and were asking Enu to steer the hide boat closer. Enu made a sharp turn, nearly taking on water over one dipping side.

The whales would show them the way to the long summer. If they were truly his people's brothers, they would not deny the humans help.

What if old Nau knew the way? Maybe that was where she had come from. . . . She couldn't really have been born out of the rocks, or from the wolves and wolverines. . . . Maybe she was a lost traveler, who had wandered far from the warm lands? And the whales had helped her survive?

Enu's thoughts sped and tumbled, flocked together and burst apart like birds. It was exhilarating.

The walrus herd, meanwhile, was now quite near, and the water frothed like the boiling contents of a giant cauldron. The hunters lowered the sail. The long oars rose creakingly in their wooden oarlocks, and obediently the hide boat hurtled toward the walruses.

Now they were very close. The animals, faces bristling with huge yellow tusks, had spotted them and were watching the men with hatred. Suddenly, the dominant male—an old bull with a broken left tusk, his rough hide knotty with parasites and riven with scars—changed tack and, at great speed, rammed the boat.

On another day, Enu might have reacted quickly enough to deflect the blow by turning the boat. But slow to surface from his own thoughts, he lost a critical moment; he saw the broken tusk rear up inside the belly of the boat, between the legs of the chief harpooner. Water poured in, and they began to sink.

The hunters were terror struck. Not one could swim. Their only hope was to hold on to the *pyh'pyh*; by a stroke of luck, these buoys, made from blown-up walrus intestines, and used for hauling a kill behind the boats, had already been prepared. The walrus, in his rage, stabbed the boat again and again. It shuddered helplessly, sinking farther into the icy water with each thrust. And how far they were from land!

There were five men in the boat. There were four pyh'pyh. And two men had their hands on the same buoy: Enu, and the youth named Kliau, his eyes deadened by fear. For Kliau knew well what the head man of the boat must do in a situation like theirs. When there was no hope of survival, when the hunters' native shore was only a stripe of land far in the distance, the helmsman must draw his hunting knife and kill his companions, and then himself, to spare them all needless suffering.

Now he found himself looking into the face of the man who would slay him, who had by chance been the nearest person in the boat. Kliau had reached for the closest pyh'pyh, this being no time to waste a moment choosing . . .

How beautiful life seemed! Even these scant few moments that were left before eternal oblivion. It shouldn't have made any difference, being slain now or moments later, but even so Kliau wished he had grabbed a different pyh'pyh. Would Enu falter, he who was regarded as the wisest among the people of the Shingled Spit, the font of old lore and half-forgotten custom? Enu knew the way to greet a newborn, and the rites of passage for the dying. Surely he would strike quick and true.

Enu, meanwhile, stalled for time. He knew that he must perform his sad duty, that they would never make it home . . . and yet he was unable to move. Here it was, so unexpected and so simple, the end of life. Another man, and not he, would find the way to the never-freezing seas, to the lands of long summer, where the sun shone from on high, where the whales and other warmth-loving creatures wintered.

Enu's companions, each longing to delay his impending doom, avoided his eyes as they bobbed gently but deliberately away from him.

Let the older ones be the first to say goodbye to this world, Enu decided. Take Ope, his face turned to the shore, his eyes brimming with grief and fear of certain death. He is leaving behind a wife and six children, all so young that the village will have to take care of them. Here is Rermyn, also leaving children, and a beautiful wife. She'll be looked after by his older brother. And here is Komo. . . . Fine hunters all, and strong men, jolly and skilled in loud singing and joyful dancing.

Enu shouted, "Hey, come over to me now!"

They were good people, the men from the boat. All heeded his call, and even those few who had at first tried to float away from him now accepted their fate and made for Enu, who was feeling for his sharp, long-bladed hunting knife in its sodden leather sheath.

Komo was the first to reach the headman. Enu decided not to kill him until the rest drew closer, rightly fearing that the sight of first blood would weaken the men's resolve. But as soon as they had all drawn next to the half-submerged boat, Kliau cried, "The whales are coming! A whole pod of whales, coming for us!"

Everyone turned to see where the young man was pointing. A cloud of fog, dappled with many colors, was speeding toward the survivors. Noisily the whale pod cut through the cold and viscous autumn waters.

"They are coming to help us!" shouted Kliau. "Our brothers are coming to help us! Old Nau spoke the truth—they are our blood brothers!"

Enu raised himself above his pyh'pyh and saw the whales approaching. Like a flotilla of magical ships out of legend they came—this race of giants—like a vast song rising from the depths of the sea. Hope and fear warred within Enu's breast. Disdaining the ancient custom could lead to unknown punishment. But who was there to punish the hunters? Who were the true arbiters of the fate of the coastal people?

As they came close, the whales slowed and quieted, careful not to hurt the men. They ringed around the hunters and herded them, each on his float, toward the beach. And the hunters, in their turn, did their best to stay together, to make it easier for the whales to protect them. Soon the men could make out yarangas and thin plumes of smoke rising to the sky.

The whales halted just beyond the line of the surf. There were people on the beach, watching in astonishment as their kinsmen approached, exhausted but overjoyed by their miraculous escape. Someone thought of throwing a strong hide thong into the water, and Enu grabbed on to the end.

Soon the hunters stood in a line before old Nau, streaming with seawater. The old woman looked at them solemnly, and then at the whale pod slowly retreating from the shore.

"Brothers always help one another," she told them quietly, before making her way back to the yarangas.

ے۵

Within the largest yaranga, where the folk of the Shingled Spit usually gathered together, a whale-stomach drum was ringing.

Enu, naked to the waist and accompanied by Kliau, was performing a new dance. He had named it the Dance of the Whale. The other rescued men danced and sang, too, slightly hoarsely, in praise of their seagoing brothers. The brand-new sacred song floated up through the smoke hole and wended to the beach, where, at the horizon, all but invisible in the night's darkness, the whales held their rumbling breath and listened.

Following Enu's lead, the dancing men hoisted their painted oars aloft, toward the ceiling, where among last year's deer carcasses, curing in the fragrant smoke, in a sea of warm fug and flickering firelight, floated a whale, expertly carved from dark driftwood.

A human is only human
When he has a brother, and his soul
Longs to repay his brother's kindness.
Death turned away from us,
Though it had touched us with a dark wing tip.
Whales saved us.
We give them praise
And thanks.

In the dimly lit yaranga, the song beat its wings against dry walrus hides, like giant drums. The people of the shore, listening, felt their hearts fill with gratitude and their spirits rise and rise. Not a few of them now remembered how they'd mocked old Nau's tales of whale kinship, taking her stories for the last gasps of a guttering mind, and felt ashamed.

The Sacred Dance of the Whale heralded the birth of a new custom and strengthened the people's faith in their unusual ancestry. As he sang, Enu was aware that the words of this new song kindled inside him without any thinking, and he wondered at his state, which was as if someone else was singing through him.

A brother is not just
One who resembles you.
A brother is one who feels your sorrows
And comes to your aid . . .

3

Whenever Ainau brought a piece of blue ice inside the yaranga, she carried with it a cold cloud that smelled sharply of frost and tickled the nose. In the warmth, the ice crackled like a thing alive. The children would surreptitiously touch a licked finger to its surface, to feel it "bite," leaving behind a thin film of pale skin stuck to the ice.

This was the season where everything outside was turned a deep blue by frost and twilight, and bright winter stars ventured tremulously across the dark sky, shivering and flickering in the all-consuming cold.

The only thing to occasionally break up the blue stillness of deep freeze were the yellow stains of firelight that fell through the thresholds of dwellings whenever hunters were expected to return from the winter ice. They would approach from the hummock-riven shore, skirting the tallest of the ice pileups and trailing behind them a rapidly freezing track of tamped snow and scattered red drops of blood.

They kept their sights on the yellow lights of home, glowing from stone lamps packed with moss and blubber, as they walked through the all-encompassing silence that hung over the Shingled Spit and its scattering of yarangas, half-buried in snow and very small indeed in the great wide world.

Kliau, looking up, could see the stars beginning their dance above—far away, the gods were about to feast, the gleam of their multihued fires mirrored in the sky. The world that seemed so empty at first was in fact densely populated. The wide, spacious sky; the far-off mountain ranges; even the dour, bare crags: they were all full of life, unknown creatures, and magical powers.

With a deep sigh, Kliau hurried onward, to the home where his wife and three children—two boys and a girl—would be waiting. Though he was tired and cold, it warmed him to the core to picture the expectant looks of their little faces; the especially keen and penetrating eye of his eldest son, Armanto; and his wife's loving solicitude.

At the yaranga, Ainau picked up a slim wooden ladle, scooped up some water—not forgetting the floating bit of ice—and went outside. She waited by the threshold, watching Kliau weave among the hummocks. She could pick him out from a dozen hunters, simply by his walk, from any distance.

Her heart glowed with warm tenderness to think of him—her husband, her Kliau—who even now was returning home with a kill. The Great Love that had breathed the coastal people into existence and turned a whale human lit up her joyful face.

Unhurriedly Kliau approached, shrugging off the harness he had used to drag the dead nerpa without a word. Ainau poured water over the dead seal's face, giving it drink, and passed the ladle to her husband, while she herself dragged the animal inside and laid it on a piece of walrus hide.

The children ringed around the nerpa, chattering excitedly. They would have to wait for it to thaw before their mother could begin to butcher it.

Kliau set to painstakingly knocking snow from his torbasses and hanging up his cleaned hunting gear, while Ainau busied herself mashing frozen meat from the storage pit in a large stone mortar, mixing it up with blubber and seasoning it with fermented greens. This was not the main dish, however—the star attraction would be the fresh nerpa meat, soon to be boiled up. As soon as the seal had thawed enough, Ainau cut it apart, reserving the skin and blubber.

The children licked their lips and waited. Finally, their mother plucked the eyes from the whiskery nerpa head, punctured them with her knife, and handed one to each of the boys, who sucked on the delicacy with moans and groans of delight, and gave their little sister a taste as well.

Kliau divested himself of all his clothing, naked apart from a small fawnskin loincloth. While Ainau butchered the seal, several visitors arrived from neighboring yarangas, and each wife left with a piece of meat. This made the family happy, for sharing good fortune, goodwill, and food was the first duty of the whale people, and a pleasant one at that.

It was often hard to imagine at the high peak of winter that summer would ever come—and that the pebbled beach would lie free of snow, the deeply blanketed tundra hills show grass green again, wide streams of free-flowing water run down the mountainsides, and the great silence of the polar night give way to bright birdsong. The sea would one day break free of ice, and the whales would come once more . . .

The family finished their repast with an uncomfortable but nevertheless pleasant feeling of satiety. Once everyone had settled back on the soft deerskins, the head of the household began to tell a tale, as was customary in every yaranga after a feast. Children must be taught about their past, so that they need never feel alone in the great wide world. Kliau's low voice cut through the warm air of the yaranga, thick with the smells of fresh blood, cooked meat, and the acrid nerpa blubber guttering in the stone lamp.

"Once, long ago, coldness and darkness covered all that was, and there was no telling earth from water or sky. Everything was dark and indistinct, as in a blizzard."

Kliau's small children lay beside him, listening with bated breath to the story of their people's ancient past.

"Not a single ray of sunlight shone through the thick clouds, heavy with moisture. But then a woman appeared. She walked over the cold, bare earth, and green grass grew from her warm footsteps. She turned to look around—she smiled—and the sun, breaking through the dank, low clouds, answered with a blazing burst of light that dispersed the gloom and spread warmth over the world. Now the woman saw that there was land and water, sky and cliffs, a shingled spit to divide the lagoon from the sea. There were gophers living in their burrows, sables wandering about the hills, birds flying over the sea . . . and the sea itself was replete with life, teeming with swimmers and divers. The woman went about the shore, living on berries and seaweed. She did not know she was human, for she had no one that she might speak with.

"That is, until Great Love came to her. Great Love turned a whale into a man, and he took the first woman to wife.

"The woman gave birth to baby whales. They lived in the lagoon at first, but when they outgrew that home, they swam up the Pilkhun Strait to meet their whale kindred and live on the open sea. After that, the woman gave birth again and again, but this time to human children. These children were our ancestors, the very first people of our tribe."

Kliau paused, then said, with feeling: "And our very own Nau, she is that first woman! She lives among us, and we revere her!"

Drifting off to the last words of the story, Kliau's children dreamed of the impossibly long-ago, mythical time when a whale could turn into a man, and a person could live on berries and seaweed. They had heard this legend more than once and, too, the story of Kliau's own miraculous rescue by whales.

They grew up watching the Sacred Dance of the Whale,

and had instruction in it, in readiness for the day that they, too, would dance in thanks and exultation among the brave hunters that gathered in the Great Yaranga.

رله

Each daybreak saw Kliau depart for the sea ice, leaving behind the Shingled Spit and its yarangas, sunk deep in snowdrifts, with only the puffing smoke holes to hint at the life and warmth kindled within.

The bluish light would grow tinged with rose as he went on, as though full sun was about to spill from the southerly sky, instead of the red glow of a sun that never showed above the horizon.

As he skirted the big hummocks and picked his way carefully across the patches of new ice, Kliau pondered the past, not for the first time. Say that you believed the story of the whale turning into a man. . . . Why had the things that happened so long ago never happened again?

So much of what lay within the ancient tales was strange and incomprehensible. Kliau even once quizzed Enu about it, only to receive the stern reply that the harder to understand such a tale was, the truer it was, and therefore the worthier of faith.

Still: why could the world not be just as clear and clean as the first breath of cold winter air after the heavy, warm morning closeness of the polog?

The starry sky, like the earth, was peopled with a multitude of creatures: hunters, maidens, deer. Human imagination had filled in the lines tracing the stars into constellations, illuminating the lives of the celestial-dwellers. You might think that this was where the dead went, but apparently not! The dead departed through the clouds, but they went to live in yet another world, one whose location was hidden even from wise men like Enu. As for Kliau, he looked up at the shining dots overhead and thought, privately, that the sky was like a great drumhead—a giant *rettem*—stretched over the earth, pierced with holes through which the rain and snow got in. Elsewhere beneath this tent there lived other nations. And the smoke from their fires rose into the sky to form clouds, shutting out the sun and bringing on bad weather.

How could the world around him be so different from the one in the legends? Unless the wise men deliberately kept everything hazy, to hide their own ignorance . . .

Farther and farther he walked over the shackled sea. All around him unfurled a breathtaking vista of chaos clothed in ice. Enormous hummocks reared up from frozen sea to sky. Among them were chunks of calved iceberg, of a white so pure it glowed blue, as if from within. Some of them had cave-like indentations—terrifying anyone who ventured inside with a soft, eerie crackling sound, like an unseen stranger walking overhead in soft, bearskin-soled torbasses.

At first glance, even the wild icescape looked homogenous, but this was not so; up close, the hummocks could be surprising. And venturing far out from shore, out where the strong sea currents broke up the ice, you would encounter nerpa. Quietly gliding in and out of black water holes that billowed with pale mist, they gazed at the blue-white world with large, round eyes.

Once out to sea, it was hard to make out the yarangas left behind on the pebbled beach, even if you climbed atop a tall hummock. They appeared as black flecks, like rabbit droppings in the snow, and beyond them sat the frozen lagoon, measureless. But looking south, hills rolled like waves toward the faraway blue mountains, and the land went on just as endlessly as the sea.

The winter sun meandered, hidden, beyond the toothy peaks of the Far Ridge. What else lay beyond those peaks?

The deer-herder people who wintered in the foothills were but distant kin to the shore people. They had splintered off a long time before, in days which only Nau could remember.

Kliau used to think that as he grew older, life's mysteries, and the things that the elders left unsaid, would be revealed. Knowledge that grown, steady hunters could be trusted with was no good for a callow youth. But now he believed that, on the contrary, these mysteries could ignite the kind of curiosity that drove a person into the unknown.

Wasn't that what was happening to Enu? Some people went so far as to say he'd gone mad, for no rational man would have gone on and on about some distant land where the summer sun spent four times as many days in the sky, where summer was so long that no sooner was it over than there came the first stirring of spring again.

"It is not just another fable," Enu had insisted. "I'm convinced that this land exists, and you and I will find it. Do you remember that terrible day we almost perished? That's when I first thought of the warm lands. Who knows? Maybe it was the whales who put the idea in my mind."

Each time Enu spoke like this, Kliau grew more determined to join him.

The people gathered around a big hide boat resting on a patch of spring ice. The ice was old and pockmarked by the sun's rays, but the boat, newly clad in a covering of semitranslucent, freshly tanned hide, thrummed at the touch, like a gigantic yarar drum. Enu was finally setting out on his incredible, long-plotted journey—and Kliau was coming with him. The third man to go was Komo, a lazybones who was always joking around but was also an expert at making images of things he had seen in drawings on the stony cliffs.

Old Nau was among those seeing them off. Her face had grown more deeply tanned, just as the yaranga roofs darkened after weathering the winter freeze, snowfall, blizzards, and fierce spring sun.

Kliau had not anticipated how terrible it would be, saying farewell to his family and friends, his wife and children, the whole of the Shingled Spit and the view from his front door, the nearby hills and crags. It was like a big stone had fallen hard onto his heart, and he nearly cried out with the pain of it.

The stone lay heavy upon him while they sailed along the ice shelf still attached to the shore and past the tall cliffs, which Kliau used to climb to contemplate the jagged peaks in the distance and wonder what lay beyond. The task ahead called not merely for faith in the old tales but for them to venture forth and see for themselves the faraway place of the long sun, where the whales—their ancestors—lived.

It had been hard to leave his wife, and especially hard to leave his children. At the last minute, he suddenly thought of those blissful early days when he had resolved to bring Ainau into his yaranga, and the two of them would walk far beyond the village, into the tundra hills, where the grass was so soft and tender . . .

The villagers gazed at the receding boat as it grew dimmer and dimmer in the light, the way a dying person dissolves in endless eternity. A dying person is exactly what many of the villagers were thinking of, as all stood in silence.

Old Nau watched the villagers for a little while, then said, with force: "This is the call of our ancestors. For whales are eternal wanderers, endlessly traversing the measureless seas. Just so, humans cannot live forever in the same place. First they invented boats, to tame the great waters and return to their beginnings . . ."

"What, and soon someone will take to the skies?" one of her neighbors interjected.

Nau did not rise to the mockery. "And why not?" she mused. "Why shouldn't that happen? For now, let the sons of whales sail the sea and discover new and unknown things. Only then will humans feel that they are truly alive."

She went on like this for a long time after, and since the men's departure was fresh in their minds, the villagers listened attentively to her words.

But time passed. Other events came and went, obscuring the memory of the three madmen who had followed in the wake of the whales to search for the long summer. Only their relatives still spoke of them, and then only while honoring the dead, who had departed through the clouds forever.

Old Nau's tales grew wearisome. The villagers humored her, but solely because it was a sacred duty to show courtesy to the old lady who had outlived time itself.

Kliau's children grew up. If ever anyone told the story of the three madmen who went on a long journey, it was as a kind of legend, half-forgotten.

ﻼ

No one measured the passing of time back then; it was obvious. Folk marked it in people's faces, in the birth and maturing of children who would one day grow old and depart through the clouds themselves.

One clear winter day, as the low, cold sun arced its shivery rays far over the hummock-riven sea, three dots appeared among the hills on the lagoon side of the spit. The dots grew larger as they approached the yarangas, but one could tell even from a distance that these were not the deer herders, who were recognizable by their bowlegged gait. Neither were these visitors from the far side of the lagoon, for they always arrived on dog sledges, in a tumult of noise.

No, these travelers walked slowly. A few times they even paused to scan the shoreline.

Every inhabitant of the Shingled Spit came outside to watch, and as the strangers came ever closer, unease crept into the villagers' hearts. The travelers were oddly dressed, in garments very unlike those of the coastal people, marked by the traces of long, arduous adventures. And another disquieting thing: the men were by no means young, but were instead of an age when people didn't go journeying without pressing need.

The travelers came closer still. Their weathered, deeply lined faces shone with joy.

One of the old village men, dressed in white deerskin pants

to signal his readiness to pass through the clouds, greeted them: "Who are you, and where are you headed?"

The travelers were silent. They scanned the faces of the crowd, as if looking for people they knew.

And then an old woman, who had stood painfully squinting at one of them with her failing eyes, cried out in a loud and terrible voice: "Kliau! It's Kliau, my husband! I know this man!" And then they all knew that these travelers were the men whose journey had passed into legend, the ones who had gone mad with the idea of learning the paths of whales.

"So you've returned," old Nau said to Enu, who was now a white-haired, shrunken old man, his eyes shining with wisdom and warmth.

They led the travelers toward the yarangas. As they walked, the men gazed deeply around them, as though imbibing the essence of their native home, of which they had dreamed for so long.

"We have journeyed across wondrous lands," Enu began. "We saw fire-breathing mountains, and marveled that those who live among them spoke our language and honored whales as their ancestors as well. They believe that the true homes of the whales lie inside their mountains, like yarangas, and that we were seeing the fire and smoke from the whales' hearths. Our distant kinsmen told us many stories of the whales. They told us that whales have the same kind of family life that humans do, and speak to one another in their own language, just as we do. They even quarrel, though very rarely—and it makes the earth shake. The smoke from their giant hearths thickens, and sometimes burning rocks shoot out from the peaks also, because the whale wives are too busy quarreling to tend to the fires properly!"

The travelers took turns telling their story. When one of them tired, another took over, and then the third. Old Nau sat among the villagers and listened too. Each of the returnees wondered that she had outlived so many and yet remained as indomitable as when they'd left her many years before.

"In those first of the far lands, we never saw the beasts that we here are used to hunting," Kliau told the assembly. "There were no walruses, and bears never venture there either. There isn't much ice to speak of, in truth, just a narrow strip by the shore, and beyond it the dark, streaming water of the free sea. People in those parts live by deer herding and fishing, which isn't food you could grow tall on, sure, but there is an inexhaustible supply of fish in the rivers. The people even feed it to their dogs."

Now Enu took over. "We followed the sun, for our first aim was to reach the lands of the long sun, where the earth remains swathed in warmth. We saw real trees, covered in green leaves, their rustling branches like the arms of giants. The trees spread over enormous distances, and it's hard to imagine how men can live in that green murk, or how they ever find their way toward the rivers and sea. We were wary of going too far into the forests, and tried to keep to the coast, always mindful that the paths of whales are sea paths."

"When we first saw the fire-breathing mountains," said Komo, "we thought we had reached the gates of the whale homelands, but we still needed to find a way inside. We didn't see whales anywhere near there, which was strange. So we carried on, getting across watery parts with the aid of the natives, as our boat was by that time in tatters and useless. At last we came across a people who could no longer make out our speech. But most of those that we met treated us as brothers, and didn't harass us."

"Not everywhere was like that, though," Enu sighed. "In one place, where people live by gathering plants in summer and raising animals whose milk they drink like water, some armed men seized us and locked us up in a special house of gloom and shadows. They kept us there for several years, enough time that we began to understand their language. They never lost their suspicion of us, saying that we were changelings who had come to their land to do them harm—and yet they did not kill us, fearful of bringing even greater disaster upon themselves.

"They fed us plants, and at first this kind of diet weakened us thoroughly, but eventually we got used to it, and regained our strength.

"One day they led us out—we had been so long in darkness that we could barely keep our eyes open in the bright sunlight—and took us inside a huge yaranga made of piled-up stones. An important man waited for us there, wanting to know where we had come from and what our intentions were.

"So we answered this curious man that we were descendants of whales, traveling along whale paths to discover the lands of much warmth and little coldness, where the sun and the migratory birds went to spend the winter.

"The important man listened to us carefully, then asked how we knew of our ancestry. We told him then that our first ancestress—old Nau, who gave birth to all our tribe—still lived among us in our village.

"This caused great tumult with the people of the warm lands. The man explained to us that they, too, descended from whales, but that the tales of ancient times were regarded almost as fairy tales. Many among them no longer believed that the ancestress of all the coastal people still lived."

Ainau, Enu's elderly wife, gazed at him happily, seeing not the silver-haired old man but the young husband who had set off on a momentous journey.

"They told us the legend of their origin, and as they spoke we heard the voice of old Nau and the words we learned in childhood. And the people told us that they were bound by an ancient promise that while brother honored brother, helped him and cared for him, that while love and accord existed between people, somewhere in the world the ancestress of all human beings, the Whale's Wife, would still live and breathe."

"We carried on," said Komo, "because we wanted to know endless warmth. We cut through giant grasses and forded rivers that that ran with water warm as walrus blood. The sun was always high overhead there, and the snow would melt overnight, though the people that lived there considered even that snowfall a real torture. They came in droves to gawk at us sweating in the heat, which they held to be cold weather."

"Further still the whale path continued," said Enu. "They swam on into the warm fogs, their spouts sparkling. But we had only strength enough for the return journey, for we knew well that what we had discovered belonged not just to us but to all of you, part that we are of a great whole of the shore people. We had seen much and reached the edge of the world. From the people we met, we knew that there was no winter in the lands still further, only an endless summer. But that life was not for us. We turned back."

"We hurried home," Kliau told them, "longing to see familiar faces, to hear the half-forgotten voices that reached us only in dreams. Our native land drew us back just as the whales are drawn to cold waters with each coming of spring."

It took several evenings for the travelers to finish their tale of adventures and meetings with other tribes, strange customs, foods, and animals. The villagers heard, silent and amazed, how in some lands people had never seen snow and would hardly believe that water could harden into stone, or that raindrops could fall as fluffy white flakes from the sky.

When the flow of storytelling at last began to ebb, and the three men started to lapse into silence, old Nau spoke once again. "Now that you have seen new lands, strange tribes, and unfamiliar beasts, tell us: What land did you think was the most beautiful?"

The men looked at one another, and Kliau gave answer. "It's true that we have seen much. But we have also learned a deep truth, and it is this: there is nothing more beautiful than your native land, the place of your birth, where your near and dear ones are, where ancient tales are told in the tongue of your childhood."

In the quiet yaranga, these words rang out like the wings of a magical bird bearing tidings.

"That is exactly as I thought," Nau told them. "Beauty lies in that which is beside you. And so the whales always return when the ice retreats, because these shores are their home, just as they are ours."

ﻋﻠﻪ

Enu had grown old and infirm and Komo was only good for making sketches of what he could remember, so it fell to Kliau to compose and perform the Dance of the Journeyer.

No one knew how many years they had spent on their travels. But though his hair was gray, Kliau had held on to his strength. He outlived his companions, dying in extreme old age and mourned by all his relations.

Old Nau was the one who dressed him for the end. Her hair silvery-gray, her face nearly black, like tanned walrus skin, but overall unbent, she made her way to the yaranga where grief and sadness now reigned, and asked everyone to leave. Kliau lay clad in white kamuss pants and white kukhlianka, ready to make his final journey.

Without a word, Nau went inside the polog and lifted the piece of bearskin from the dead man's face. In death, Kliau looked tranquil and serene.

Old Nau asked for a *vykvepoigyn* to be brought to her, and they brought in the polished, slightly crooked stick, dented in the middle where the stone knife used for scraping hides would be placed. The crone placed one end of the stick beneath the dead man's head and began to talk to him, her voice never above a whisper. She asked him detailed questions and awaited answers. These were short but unambiguous. The deceased wished to take along a pair of sturdy torbasses and his hunting spear.

Quietly the old woman relayed his wishes, and a little pile of objects grew by the dead man's head. He would be taking these things with him as he went through the clouds.

The men carried him to Funerary Hill. And life went on. A new spring was coming, the sun rising high over the snows to light up the tundra and icebound sea.

5

Enu's grandson Givu was a fragile and thoughtful young man. One day he came to Nau, asking, "What is the secret of your eternal life?"

The old lady looked up sharply at his boldness. This was a sacrilegious thing to ask, and unexpected. "There's no secret, and there's no eternal life either," she told him.

"But you go on living," the youth persisted. "So there is both eternal life and a mystery."

"I go on living . . ." mused Nau. The answer came to her even as she spoke, from some strange place. "I go on living because Great Love is alive in the world."

"Then, if it died, you too would die?"

"Great Love is eternal," said Nau.

Givu fell silent, thinking.

Nau watched him and wondered what made him this way. Was he afflicted by his own name? It must be hard living with a name like "All-Knowing," though the giving of names was deliberate, parents trying to mark out a path for their children. In fact, Nau had named Givu herself, for he was the blood descendant of Enu, who had first dreamed of following the paths of whales to learn about the world.

"I have many doubts," Givu sighed. "They eat at me."

In parting, Nau gave him this advice: "Try not to ask so many questions. Think things through for yourself."

و۔

Autumn came, and with it the walrus herd arrived to take up their breeding grounds beneath the cliffs. For several days

Givu watched them mating and felt as if he, too, was in heat. It was all he could do not to throw himself at the first available woman—and as bad luck would have it, the women were all nearby, picking berries and rummaging through animal burrows in search of edible roots. But Givu fought the feeling. He had a vague but strong sense that the answers to his questions lay elsewhere.

He went to the tundra. There, he wandered about in the silence of the cooling days. He peered into clear streams where fish swam stately by, slowly waggling their fins. The water-dwellers' gray-blue bodies looked like the images that had been carved into the cliffs by Komo, come to life.

Givu slaked his thirst in the water, bending down to study his own reflection. A long, drawn, wide-eyed face looked back at him. He had been told that he resembled his celebrated grandfather, Enu. But that was as far as the resemblance went; Enu, of course, had found an outlet for his insatiable curiosity and had gone on a journey that lasted most of his lifetime. Were Givu to follow in his footsteps, all he would find was what Enu, Komo, and Kliau had already seen.

So where to go?

And where did it all begin—the very endlessness of the world, the clouds over the tundra and the green grass that turned yellow each and every autumn?

Where did the flowers, blue like shards of sky, come from? The red berries and the water currents that carried silent, tranquil fish? The animals and birds, the beasts of the sea? Could the origins of human beings really be as simple as old Nau would have him believe?

And, worst of all, why did these questions burn inside him so, waking him at night and driving sleep away, whispering things that made no sense, filling his mind with the crazy idea of killing old Nau?

A stiff and steady wind pulsed over the tundra, raising waves across the yellow grass, just like a sea.

Givu strode across the land, hopping over springy tufts of moss and leaping across rivulets and streams. He never tired; the wind seemed to him a pair of wings that carried him over the earth. He waited for the feeling that Nau had spoken of, back when she was young and didn't know the whale Reu, that feeling of oneness with the natural world. Givu wanted to be the wind and the stream and the sleepy fish in that stream, as Nau had been; to be the grass and the hillock, the molting old sable fox, the slim crane patrolling his raspberry-strewn bog, the gopher and the mouse dragging a sweet *pelkumren* root back to its nest . . .

But nothing of the kind happened. He did stub his toes painfully a few times on rocks concealed in the lush grass, and his foot ached, distracting him and breaking the flow of his thoughts.

What if Nau had also felt nothing?

What if she was just making it all up?

Maybe even the epic voyage into the distant warm lands, where the sun roamed tirelessly above the earth and people raised food from the ground, eating grasses just like the tundra deer do—maybe that never really happened either? There had always been those who doubted. Didn't Enu set off on that very journey because he, too, had always doubted?

Givu sat down on a hillock. The scent of dry autumn herbs was making him a little light-headed. Soon this smell would fill the yaranga, carried indoors with the heaps of dead grass the women would gather in preparation for winter, reminding them all of the green world of summer, warm and beautiful with flowers.

Most people lived perfectly well without prying into the causes of things, without puzzling over the mysteries of the natural world. Why did he, Givu, have to be the one to struggle with it all?

His thoughts turned once more to women. They were strange creatures. Why had they been made different from men? Was it really just so the human race might continue, and to give men pleasure? Why was it that the purest happiness one could experience was linked to the expectation of new life? And did it follow, then, that taking life, killing someone . . . would the taker of life experience the opposite? Yet life was brighter and more joyful than death, so the feeling it brought must be the stronger . . .

Givu looked around afresh, eyes blazing with discovery. One of the mysteries was unraveling to him and lay tantalizingly close, almost within his grasp . . .

Flushed with excitement, he sprang up and ran back toward the village, yarangas just visible on the sea side of the lagoon, mere specks on the beach.

He couldn't wait to test his theory.

༄

The woman was crouching by the stream, filling a hide pouch with *kukunet* leaves; strange, how those leaves had the same name as a woman's own hidden parts. Givu stopped a way off, and as he drank in her every move, a torrid heat began to overtake him. In his mind's eye, he was already running his hot palms over her body, tearing off her fur-lined kerk'her.

Losing all control, he came at her like a wakened brown tundra bear. The bag dropped from her hand and rolled down the hill.

$\mathcal{e}\mathcal{l}$

"You frightened me," said the woman, after. Givu had let her go with a moan of disappointment, for there was no sign of the happiness that would herald the beginning of his new life.

"Tell me, what did you feel when I took you?" Givu asked.

"I've just told you," the woman said. "Only fright. You didn't give me a chance to feel anything else."

"It's my own fault, then," Givu mused regretfully, rising from the cold, hard earth.

What had happened? He'd wanted the woman so badly. He would have gone through fire and water for her, in that moment of wanting—and yet as soon as his blazing desire was satisfied, he felt let down, like a man who tries to quench his thirst with freshly fallen snow.

He walked away from the woman. She dusted herself off and started down the slope, to gather up her spilled and crumpled kukunet leaves.

6

They had hunted walrus on their breeding-ground beaches, prepared the kopal'khen and stashed it in meat pits on the shadowed side of the lagoon, and traded blubber-filled skin bags with the deer people in return for meat and hides. Now it was time to prepare for the Whale Festival.

Time to stretch tanned walrus stomachs over round wooden tambourine frames, shaped over steam and furnished with walrus-tusk handles. Time to paint designs onto ceremonial oars, illustrating the old tale of how whales saved the hunters at sea. Time to make up new songs and dances, to fashion festive clothing and dye deerskins with red ochre from the foot of the Far-off Crags.

On the appointed day, the people of the Shingled Spit were awakened by the long-familiar tumult of an approaching whale pod. The sound of their coming filled the air all the way from the crust of ice encroaching from the sea to the crags pounded endlessly by ocean waves, the water now sluggish and thick with the cold.

At dawn, everyone, including the elderly and the children, went down to the beach. They carried dishes piled with red shrimp, broken-up starfish, seashell shards and bits of crab claw, dried-out mollusks, and shreds of seaweed. Everything was liberally dressed in nerpa fat.

The white-haired old men creakily belted the songs from the beginnings of their tribe—the time of the legendary Father Whale, Reu—and the women and youths sang along. The ocean fairly boiled with whale spouts, and a sparkling mist hung in the air above them.

At the oldest man's sign, the people threw their offerings into the water. As though they, too, followed a signal, the whales thanked their land brothers as one with a watery cascade high into the air, then made their stately annual procession toward the shores where the water never froze in winter, following the path known to them since time immemorial.

Givu joined the others in throwing in the sacramental food, which no one would ever think of eating themselves. But as he sang, he wondered, privately, as he often did now, what gave his people their unshakable faith in these nonsensical proceedings.

At sunset, the largest yaranga rang with the sound of tambourines. Each man performed the Dance of the Whale, hoping to outdo the others in the art of expressing feeling and mood.

Givu slowly pulled on a pair of special dance gloves. Silhouettes of baby whales decorated the black nerpa skin, and when the dancer wiggled his fingers or twitched his hand, the whales seemed to be swimming in dark water.

Whenever he danced, moving in time with the drumbeats, Givu experienced an astonishing sense of expansion. It was as though he was growing taller, wider—stretching to fill the entire yaranga, then whooshing out through the smoke hole to spill across the whole of the Shingled Spit, ranging over the bay and the lagoon and the cliffside grottoes, still full of last year's snow, now turned to dark ice. His heart grew with him, and his lungs. There was not air enough for them inside the yaranga. He danced in the thrall of his own feelings, unaware of the men around him as drumbeats and singers' voices reverberated through him.

Now he suddenly saw, clear as day, the eyes of the woman he had taken by the stream, the one he had thought to start his new life with. He didn't know what had come over him then, or how—his desire had made him blank to everything else, the sky and the earth, even the hard, stony ground.

An unfamiliar warmth kindled inside him, like someone patiently, lovingly stoking a fire in his breast, fanning it with careful breath.

Givu's hands danced before his face, and through his moving fingers, through the baby whales swimming in a dark sea, he saw the eyes of that woman. With a mounting sense of joy, he strained to absorb this growing tenderness and warmth. It was a new kind of feeling—not the blazing, furious flame of desire, but more like a quiet song, like flickering firelight over a sweep of snow.

مۇ

When the first snows came, Givu set up his own yaranga, separate from his parents', and installed the woman in it. From then on, she was his wife.

In the heat of their passionate nights, Givu looked for that highest joy that signified the start of new life, but no matter how hard he tried, it didn't happen.

Frustrated and disappointed, he would wander into the tundra and rove among the hills, sometimes going so far that he only made it back home toward morning. He spent much time alone with his thoughts, which buzzed about his head like mosquitoes, appearing and vanishing with no regard to his own wishes. These thoughts—these questions—were strange and insistent, and there was no brushing them aside anymore. They had to be answered.

Old Nau came to them late one evening and made herself comfortable in a corner of the yaranga. As was her custom, she lived like a nomad, moving from one yaranga to the next.

She counseled Givu's wife about tanning hides and making clothes, about the kind of sinews that made for the best thread, about smoking nerpa flippers so you could pull the skin off as easily as a glove. But Givu heard the crone's voice as if in a stupor, a single thought beating about his head like a caged bird: Could she really be immortal?

Givu woke in the night, in a cold sweat. He felt for his sharply honed knife in the darkness, imagining the blade cutting into her wiry neck, almost crunchy with moving parts. He imagined her black blood staining the white deerskin bedcovers. He could even hear the old woman's death rattle as she let out her last breath, as her endless life flew up and away into the blue sky, through the winter clouds, glinting with moonshine and the polar lights.

Desperate to evade these grim imaginings, Givu looked for distraction. He pressed himself close to his wife, whose soft skin radiated heat. Obediently she moved closer to him, opening to meet him, like a spring tundra flower.

Now—now, at last—Givu felt it. The secret and long-awaited thing he had yearned for . . . the vast, slowly dissipating feeling of tenderness, a lingering, sweet pain deep inside him. And as the pain left him, he was suffused with a strange contentment that lifted him bodily and then rushed him down again, the wind whistling in his ears, just like when he was a boy sledging down one of the foothills to the edge of the snow-covered lagoon.

This time Givu was certain of kindling new life. His thoughts of old Nau and immortality seemed silly and trivial now. With a rueful smile, he left the yaranga for the bracing, fresh air of the winter night.

He went into the tundra once more, light on the wings of

a new joy and a new song bursting from his breast, out of the great tenderness that had filled him to the brim. What if this was the Great Love that Nau always talked about? What if he was now part of it, the Great Love that had revealed itself to him, rewarding him for his patience and determination?

The thick blue haze that lay before Givu slowly transmuted into a glittering, star-bright sky. To the north, polar flares—a sign that the whales were feasting in their underground palaces—danced above the slumbering humans.

Givu crossed the lagoon and wound his way through the gently sloping hills toward sunrise. Soon he was at the foot of the Far-off Crags. He had walked far and would have walked farther still. But a voice stopped him in his tracks: "Stand and look around you!"

Givu obeyed.

Everything was as it had been, and he couldn't discern anything new or different. The same stars hung in the sky, only they were a bit dimmer, now that sunrise was close at hand. And the polar lights had ceased.

"And now? How do you see things now?"

The voice was immensely strange, coming from everywhere at once. It filled the world around, above, and below, no matter where Givu turned to look. But Givu was somehow unsurprised by the voice. It was as though he had expected it all along.

Once more he cast his gaze about, as the voice commanded. He realized that his vision was indeed somehow clearer, as though a fog had lifted from his eyes. All things stood out in sharp relief: each fold of wind-polished snow and the subtle changes of color wrought upon them by the lightening sky; each pebble and blade of grass poking out of the snowdrifts. He could smell the river ice, both near and far, and the scent of the frozen earth, aching unbearably under its thick coat of snow.

"From now on you will hear and see far more than an ordinary man!"

Thus spoke the unseen voice, and Givu's newly keen ear marked how it diminished like a mountain echo, evaporating into thin air.

An urgent question beat in Givu's breast: "Who are you? Why did you choose me and no one else? Why did you say nothing of old Nau's mystery?" But he went back to the village. At his yaranga, his wife looked up at him with quiet wonderment; never before had she seen him so calm and serene, so at peace with his unruly thoughts.

From then on, Givu always returned home with a kill. It was as if his feet knew just where to be when the cautious nerpa surfaced onto the ice. His luck was noted among the villagers, and soon people were coming to him for his views on hunting. To his own surprise, Givu was always sure of his answers and spoke good sense.

In time, people began to approach him for many reasons, even when a child or dog was taken ill. So Givu gave counsel and supplied folk with remedies made of herbs, often also containing different bits of sea life, like polar bear bile and black, coagulated lakhtak blood.

There were times that Givu felt the need of the voice himself. Then he would take up the tambourine, dampen its humming surface, and douse the polog fire. He would sing, occasionally pausing to listen.

The words of his song came from beyond, and he never questioned this nor tried to puzzle out their source. Old Nau's deep, bottomless gaze still troubled him sometimes, but these days all he had to do was think of something else and thoughts of her vanished.

Slowly, imperceptibly, Givu had become the most well-known and important person in the village, and people felt compelled to consult him before any serious undertaking. They began to call him "Enenyl'yn," which means "the one who heals."

Givu's wife gave him a sturdy brown boy who, as soon as he was born, let out a loud and demanding holler. Old Nau wiped him down with blue spring snow and swaddled him in a soft fawnskin. She dusted his navel with ashes of burnt tree bark and placed the stone blade she'd used to cut the cord in a hide purse, stowing it away in a hidden place.

"Like a baby whale, he is," she liked to say, delighting in the infant's shiny, smooth skin.

The voices foretold good fortune for the newborn; Givu's happy heart was full to bursting with affection for him. "Perhaps this is the wings of Great Love that I feel," he wondered aloud at one evening's meal.

But the old lady silently shook her head. "Great Love stretches its wings over all people," she said. And then she added, "If it was not merely satisfaction with your own deeds in your heart, then one might say that you have learned what Great Love is."

An unheard-of disease came down upon the village. People began to have trouble with their eyes and lose their appetite. For days they would lie inside their yarangas, indifferent to everything, until quietly they left through the clouds.

The men were quick to take all the dead to Funerary Hill, but the unfed, starving dogs dragged gnawed arms and legs, and even heads, back to the village.

Finally, the baffled people came to Givu. "You are our last hope," they told him.

Givu fell silent, not knowing what to say to the despairing, frightened villagers. He was himself aghast and worried. Each morning he listened to his small son's breath, dreading to see the signs of disease. He felt as though he was always carrying with him the most fragile of vessels, filled with precious liquid: the essence of all his love for his new life and for the boy.

"We know that you can see and hear better than anyone," the people said to him. "And so we put our hopes in you."

Givu dressed carefully, pulling over his fur kukhlianka a long suede robe decorated with colorful deerskin strips. He wore low torbasses, painstakingly decorated with the same motif as the ceremonial oars, on his feet. Moving deliberately, he put on a pair of warm mittens and picked up his ceremonial staff. It was made from a light, jointed piece of wood and had a disk at the bottom to keep it from piercing through the snow.

The weather was remarkably calm and still. The sun shone from the highest point in the vault of the sky. Its rays, bouncing off the glossy snowdrifts, were dazzling. Givu took out a strip of leather with two narrow slits and tied it over his eyes, to protect himself from snow blindness.

Despite the bright good weather, the Shingled Spit was eerily deserted. Even the dogs curled up outside were silent and listless, unable to muster an interest in the one man who braved the outdoors and walked past them, wielding his ceremonial staff in wide arcs.

Givu went past the last of the yarangas, crossed the flat, and found himself at the foot of the crags. Following some strange instinct, he turned toward the sea. After climbing to a low, snow-capped promontory usually covered by water, he paused and looked about.

The ground beneath the overhanging rocks was blue with deep shadow. In the other direction, ice hummocks marched away into the sea and there sat everywhere a blinding, sun-bright silence that made the mouth dry and filled a man with dread.

Just below lay the road taken by his people whenever they sledged from the village onto the sea ice or to the neighboring settlements. Usually the snow would be riven with runner marks, but today it was an untouched blanket of white.

But wait, what was that?

Some kind of insect? Flies? Mosquitoes?

What insect could live atop the snow? During the day was one thing: they might catch a bit of warmth, though they'd have to stand stock-still, facing the light, for quite a while. But the night frost was enough to drive even the thickly furred dogs to beg to be let indoors. Never mind insects . . .

Givu stooped down to look at the skittering spots, then stopped in his tracks, astonished. His heart raced in horror to see that one of the spots was a man, dressed in a kukhlianka and torbasses, a malakhai sitting jauntily on his head. A man in every sense of the word, with well-defined features, and smiling ruefully up at him, but so tiny . . . no bigger than the joint of Givu's pinkie, or perhaps smaller still. Peering at him, Givu went cold—another step and he might have crushed the little person underneath his own lakhtak-skin torbasses.

"Who are you?" asked Givu, kneeling.

"We are the *rekken*," said the man.

Givu now saw many more little people rushing toward them. They had to bridge dimples in the snow, which to them of course were deep holes, and their windmilling arms made them hard to see properly until they came close. Givu was even more astonished to see a wee sledge with a team of fly-sized dogs hurtling over to where he stood.

"What are you doing here?"

"We are carrying disease," explained the man. "We know well the grief we have caused in your village. But this is our bitter duty. We do always try to skirt human settlements, but this time a blizzard covered our tracks and caused us to lose the way. Now your people will be sick until we've traveled well past. We are much smaller than you, and the distance from the first to the last yaranga on the beach is a great one for us. Our dogs will take several days to get clear of the village. We rest at night and travel by day."

"So what's to be done?" Givu said anxiously.

"Well, we don't know what else we *can* do," sighed the man with a miniscule plume of breath.

The rekken had thin voices, like the chirping of birds, yet each word was clear.

"Are there many of you?" Givu said.

"Ten or so sledges," came the answer.

The other rekken were listening with interest. Several had even climbed onto Givu's feet to examine his torbasses and marvel at the enormous stitches.

"Why don't I drive you all past the village in my sledge?" offered Givu.

The little man was pleased with the idea. "That would be a very good thing! Just be careful with us—you're a giant, after all."

Givu promised to do his best.

"One more thing. Humans are not to know of our existence," said the man pointedly.

Givu said he understood. Returning to his yaranga at a run, he took his light sledge down from the roof and iced the runners so they'd slide more easily over the snow. He considered harnessing the dogs but decided against it; the hungry animals couldn't be trusted not to gobble up all the rekken and their gear.

Givu hastened back. He was almost anxious that he would find no trace of the little people. It was all too unlikely, especially the way they were so exactly a copy of real people. Givu remembered the puff of steam emerging from the rekken's mouth, and the thought made him both excited and uneasy. But the rekken were still there, waiting for him.

They brought over their tiny sledges, laden with some odd-looking baggage, tightly strapped on. The fly-sized dogs kept up a racket of barely audible barking, and looking at them, Givu struggled to hold back a smile.

The rekken themselves took things very seriously. They asked Givu to help them load their sledges onto his, as it was far too tall for them. Givu took off his gloves and, using only his pointer finger and thumb, gently and carefully transferred the rekken and their dogs onto his sledge. He could feel their warm bodies between his fingers, and the way their little booted feet and mittened hands moved. Peering into their grave faces, he wondered if he was about to wake up, and if the whole thing would vanish like a dream. But he didn't wake up. He carried on gingerly loading the rekken onto his sledge, placing them so they couldn't easily fall off. Finally all was ready, and he strapped himself into the harness.

He walked at the edge of the sea ice, hidden from the

yarangas' view. From time to time he looked back at his sledge; the rekken had clumped together in the middle, holding on to one another and for dear life. His keen ears picked up the dogs' whining and the little men's exclamations. So Givu walked as softly as he could and took the smoothest path, aware that a bump that might seem small to him was a full ice hummock to the rekken, and that a sharp jolt from the runners hitting hard ice might well knock the breath right out of them.

Passing the last of the yarangas, Givu headed southwest, leading the disease-carrying creatures away from the neighboring village as well. Loading them onto his sledge, Givu had tried to get a closer look at the diseases strapped to their small ones, but all was too well packed, and he had seen nothing.

He halted near the Pil'khun Strait. One of the rekken walked up the wooden slats to him with word that they would continue on alone from there.

Givu carefully unloaded the sledges, dogs, and little people. They immediately busied themselves readying the teams, untangling harnesses, and shouting at the dogs. Watching them, Givu felt awkward and somehow embarrassed, as if he were the interloper.

Once the rekken were settled on their sledges, the one who had first spoken with Givu approached his right torbass and addressed him. "We are going on our way now. We thank you for helping us, but it was your people you helped most. We try to go around, but we don't know the land all that well, and sometimes we just happen on a human place by mistake."

Givu felt emboldened to ask what the disease they carried looked like, but at this the man's face contorted in horror. Dropping his voice to a whisper, he told Givu, "That's not something anyone may know. The diseases are packed onto our sledges and we dare not unpack them. But when we pass villages, a spirit emanates from inside, striking the people down."

"Do you get sick too?" asked Givu.

"We are spared," the man said. "Otherwise, who would do the carrying?"

The rekken drove off, leaving only the faintest tracks on the snow, almost invisible unless you bent low to the ground. Once they disappeared from view, Givu couldn't help himself—he took a few steps forward, to catch up. But there was no sign of them, nor their sledge tracks, now. They had vanished into the pale blue air, shot through with sunlight.

Givu slowly walked back to the village and back to his own yaranga and *chottagin*. From the threshold he called to his wife in a loud, clear voice, "The illness has gone!"

Seeing the disbelief on the younger woman's face, old Nau chided her, "He speaks the truth."

Later, when the sun bowed over the ruddy snow and all the villagers crowded inside Givu's yaranga, the old lady told them this: "The truth is always more extraordinary than make-believe, and harder to believe in. A man may doubt his own eyes. But today you are all witnesses to a great truth: Givu has saved the people. Only chosen ones are given such gifts by fate, only the special people capable of believing things an ordinary person never could."

Part III

1

Givu had gotten old. Already he had grandsons; his son, the one he had saved from the disease brought by the rekken, was famed all along the coastline for his strength and good fortune. Givu sensed old age lying in wait for him like winter hiding behind the mountains. He was less keen to get up early in the morning and would lie in bed for a long while, head sticking out of his sleeping polog, so he could see the sky through his smoke hole. He liked to recline there, breathing cold, fresh air and ruminating on the secret of immortality. It was astonishing, but old Nau was just the same as she had ever been—all through the childhood, youth, middle years, and finally, yes, old age, of the most famous and respected man on the Shingled Spit and far beyond. Neither famine, which they had faced more than once, nor frost, nor rain, nor blizzard seemed to have any effect on her.

Sure, during the sacred Whale Festival celebrations—to greet the arriving whale pods or fare them well as they left for the winter—they still secured Nau in the place of honor. But they paid about as much attention to her as they did to the ceremonial boat oars. There was no use in her at all: not in her wearisome yarns of how men came from whales, and not in her absurd insistence on being wife to the Father Whale, Reu, and on having given birth to baby whales. No one really believed that she had lived forever, because how could you possibly prove it?

Givu, on the other hand, received a stream of praise as the great man, the one who knew all, who could tell where hunting would be plentiful, forecast the weather, and heal the sick.

But Givu knew that even if old Nau were not immortal, she had already lived far longer than a normal person could. Whenever she came to live in his yaranga for a few months, Givu watched her intently, trying to puzzle out what it was that made her any different from all the other inhabitants of the Shingled Spit. The old woman was grindingly ordinary, however. She ate the same things that most very old people eat, avoiding hard-to-chew or tough food, as her teeth were ground down to stumps. She slept lightly and often woke during the night. She talked about everyday things, and if the itch to tell whale stories was in abeyance, she would gossip with the rest of the women, nattering happily about women's things. He didn't like to admit it, but Givu had even spied on her relieving herself, after her public habits and behavior proved unrevealing. It was all exactly as with other people her age, nothing special.

What was it about her, then? Givu couldn't resist trying her once more.

"People keep asking me," she said peevishly.

But Givu wasn't giving up yet. "Yes, people are curious."

"I don't consider myself especially long-lived," Nau said vaguely.

"But you're just the same as you were when I was a child, and now I am an old man myself."

"Why do you ask pointless questions, about things that don't matter?" She was really irritated now. "Don't you have other things to think about?"

"If someone tried to kill you," Givu persisted, "would you die from a wound?"

Nau looked up at him in surprise. Two dull tears rolled down her face. "Why would you say such a thing?" She stifled a sob. "You must be feeling unwell. . . . How could a person raise their hand to another person? He would cease to be human, the moment he did another person harm."

It was only later that Givu realized this question, so carelessly blurted out, was the turning point that hastened his own going through the clouds into the other world. How could he even voice such a thought? After that, whenever he caught Nau looking at him, he recognized deep compassion and pity in her eyes, no matter that for an old man he was hearty and never ill. Yet now he felt his strength ebbing from him, like a stream drying up in summertime, once the mountain snow that fed it has melted away . . .

At the end, he hadn't the strength to hate old Nau. He understood at last that no matter how filled his life had been with pleasure and respect, it was Nau who had been truly happy. Yes, this ordinary-looking, ordinary-seeming woman—she who knew the secret of immortality and Great Truth.

Tossing and turning in his bed all morning as he considered this, Givu would finally rise and go sit next to his yaranga, on a big boulder that weighed down the walrus-skin outer walls. As people passed by, they would greet him and ask for his advice.

This world would survive him—the sky, the clouds, the cliffs, and the sea—and his kinsmen would die, too, one day. But the old woman would carry on existing, just like the eternal mountains and clouds and wind and sky.

His grandson Armagirgin bounded up to him, almost upending the old man from his seat. The boy thought it uproariously funny to see his grandfather wobble and clutch at the air in alarm.

"How unkind you are," Givu chided. "Is it right to laugh at someone weaker and less able?"

"But it's so funny," Armagirgin assured him. "You look like the *kanaelgin* fish, when it's flopping around on land!"

Givu saw his child self in the boy. Unlike Givu at the same age, Armagirgin was hardy, lively, and sociable. All his inner traits were on the outside, like bright ornaments decorating a kukhlianka. Yet those traits—ambition, the yen to rule others, the pleasure in other people's obedience—they were all so familiar. Where Givu had slaked his thirst for power with long toil and determination to think through his questions, Armagirgin simply grabbed at things with both hands. Of course much of this was simply because he was the grandson of a great man.

How disappointed would he be, when inevitably he came up against the one person he could never dominate? Even if you pretended not to see Nau, not to be spooked by her very existence, still she was there among them like a silent reproach, a living conscience. She was always with them, the ancient woman who seemed to live—together with her whale tales— outside of time itself.

Looking at Armagirgin now, Givu was reminded of what the boy had said on first hearing that the sea carried his whale brothers. He had been inconsolable. "I don't want those ugly floating monsters to be my brothers," he had screamed. "They are huge and black, and they scare me!"

Old Nau watched the child with horror, muttering under her breath, probably some whale incantations of hers. They had managed to calm the boy then, but as he grew up, his feelings on the subject had not changed. Whenever someone told one of Nau's timeworn stories about the beginnings of their people, Armagirgin could be counted upon to sneer his derision for all to see.

～

When Armagirgin set off to hunt on fresh sea ice for the very first time, Givu handed his grandson a staff of jointed wood with solemn words: "Our ancestor Enu carried this staff through many faraway lands as he searched for truth."

"He find it?" said Armagirgin distractedly. He was in a hurry to be on his way.

"When he returned from his long journey, he said there is only one truth: no land is better than our homeland."

"Is that all he came back with?" Armagirgin smirked.

"He also brought back this staff, which in our family is passed down to the most able," said Givu.

Unimpressed and unmoved, Armagirgin took the staff. It was amazingly light in his hand.

"Let it bring you happiness and good fortune." Givu's voice trembled with the sense of occasion, and his over-spilling love for his grandson.

"Well, what I need first of all is to bag a kill for myself," Armagirgin replied, and he joined the other youths, who were all going sea hunting.

They returned with a rich haul; Armagirgin himself dragged back three nerpa. His companions later described how cleverly he had hunted them. Catching hold of one, he would drag it away from the ice hole, then sit astride it and ride the poor thing back to the water, hooting with laughter, before dragging it away again—and so on, and so on—until the exhausted creature laid down its head for the last time.

Everyone thought this exceedingly funny, with the exception of old Nau. She shook her head reproachfully and muttered her whale charms and spells.

لي

As soon as Givu sensed death at the threshold of his yaranga, he called for Armagirgin. His grandson was bright-eyed with his exciting life and clearly impatient to be gone from his grandfather's badly aired and gloomy polog, already rank with corruption and death.

"My grandson," said Givu solemnly. He took Armagirgin by the hand, worried that the young man would escape back to his noisy friends, leaving Givu's words unheard. "I want to tell you this before I die: you will accomplish much in your life, more even than I have. I can feel it. But I want to warn you, too—you are no one until you have solved the mystery of that old woman."

"What woman?"

"Nau."

"Oh, her!" Armagirgin dismissed her with a flick of his hand. "She's just crazy. And everything she says is boring, and always has been, because none of it is true!"

"Armagirgin . . ."

Givu tried to squeeze his grandson's hand, but his strength deserted him. The old man's spirit went up and away, straight through the smoke hole and into the clouds.

2

Oh yes, here was a real man, on whom all the coastal people and deer people could look upon with pride—and did.

Strong, handsome, tall, with a hearty voice that could dimple calm waters, was Armagirgin. He liked to say that true happiness lay in having skill and strength, so that a man could do anything he wished, and nothing was forbidden.

As a child he had mocked the women who left a bit of sweet *pelkumren* root behind when scavenging from mouse holes, or even gave the mice a piece of dried meat in recompense. "Those feeble little nobodies don't deserve to keep a thing!" He'd use a stick to excavate and break open the hidey-holes, digging out every crumb. Everything was for the pot when he fished in the lagoon; not a single small fry went back in the water.

All his actions were accompanied by bellowing words and booming laughter. People liked to be near him, because with Armagirgin everyone felt free to say whatever they wished, do whatever they felt like, and satisfy any of their desires as unceremoniously as eating or sleeping.

Little by little, people began to forget to thank the whales for helping with the hunt. Armagirgin was sure that it only looked like the whales were driving sea life toward the shore. Really the animals all came of their own volition.

Autumn came, and so did the walruses, returning to their customary breeding grounds on the shingled beach beyond the cape, foamy with frosty waves. It was decided that the men would hunt early in the morning, as soon as the sun rose.

The hunters crept up on them from the crags above and fell to killing the peacefully resting animals. They butchered everything they saw, young and old. The walruses' thick moans and the stench of killing rose up over the sea, twining with the sharp scent of the cold surf.

When the last of the walruses was dead, Armagirgin raised his bloody knife and shouted his triumph, so loudly that it startled the thousands-strong flocks of birds from their cliffside nests.

"Only we!" he yelled. "Only men are the true masters of the world! And we will take whatever we need, giving no thanks and asking no one's permission!"

In the distance, the pod of whales raised their spouts.

The villagers spent the winter lying about in a sated stupor. The underground meat pits were full to overflowing. Men only went to hunt out of a yen for nerpa meat. Each evening there was tambourine drumming within the Great Yaranga, and praiseful songs about the good luck of mankind, about the way that strong men were allowed anything they could take and hold, and how the true glory of a real man was being able to grab today's good fortune like he'd grab a beauty by her streaming, long hair.

Armagirgin took another wife, since the plentiful food gave him much potency and one woman was no longer enough. A year after the despoliation of the walrus colony he took a third.

Singers composed songs about his exploits; dancers portrayed him as a great man who had given people a true happiness. These were not songs that promised future plenty, nor vague consolation, like a desperate man tossing crumbs of dried meat to unknown gods. No, this was the kind of sated gladness that made people belch loudly and look down their noses as though they were flying suddenly above the ground.

The next autumn, the walruses did not return to their customary beach. They swam a wide berth around the Shingled Spit, and the hunters had to go far into the open sea to catch one.

This only provoked and stoked the hunters, drunk with the unspent might they'd stored through the winter's good eating. They rowed so fiercely that they could sometimes match the whales, still swimming unafraid alongside their hide boats, for speed.

"Hey you, ancestors!" Armagirgin liked to taunt them. "Show us, brothers, how fast you can swim!"

The women and old people awaited the hunters' return, to do the work of pulling walrus carcasses up onto the beach. Old Nau would stand among them. In recent years she had grown almost silent. And although she never complained about her ailments, she seemed to have grown even older.

Still living in each yaranga by turn, she always avoided Armagirgin's—while *he* would only say, with a crooked grimace, that the old woman's presence and deadly dull tales would only put him in a bad mood. But he liked to give his opinion, nevertheless.

"How can anyone really believe that these fat, silent, dumb beasts, these mountains of meat and blubber, are our brothers? You'd have to have a sick imagination to come up with that, or else a senile mind. Who else would question the great dominion of the strong man over all other creatures?"

People listened to Armagirgin's words, and while at first they only agreed secretly, in their hearts, eventually they grew accustomed to saying as much out loud. What he said was simpler and easier to understand than old Nau's strange and disquieting statements about their kinship with whales.

The villagers were proud of their Armagirgin and keen to spread his fame far and wide. Armagirgin, meanwhile, cast about for a way to spend his boundless energies.

Once he took his single-man kayak out into Irvytgyr, the narrowing gulf separated from the sea by a long sandspit with two tall mountains. Working a small double-paddled oar, he looked into the rising sun and sang a strident song:

> *I am the greatest of all creatures!*
> *There is nothing to overcome me!*
> *In the deeps of the sea, in the heights of the sky*
> *There is nothing I cannot have,*
> *If it is my desire!*

His kayak flew over the golden path marked out by the sun. The water burbled under the hull, as if singing with the hunter, and the kayak bounced along, ringing like a drum.

When the shoreline disappeared in mist, Armagirgin paused to look around. He loved going out alone, testing his strength, loved feeling the promise of all that a strong man armed with a sharp spear could do.

A nerpa's head bobbed up nearby. In a moment, Armagirgin had it harpooned, its dead body lashed to the side of his kayak. A few minutes more, and a second nerpa was lashed to the other side. But Armagirgin yearned to do something unusual, something special, to show off his prowess.

He would have liked a stiff wind, the better to battle the waves and feel the power of nature and best it. Such contests made a man stronger, his vision keener. Yet the cloudless sky and silence promised serenity and good weather.

Armagirgin flipped the double-paddled oar to and fro in his hands; he made the kayak spin. But there was no one to see and admire his power and skill, except for a whale pod playing nearby. Armagirgin, filled with the familiar loathing, spent some time shouting insults in their direction.

The sun began to dip to the horizon. Armagirgin, too, headed home, leisurely parting the water with his oar.

As the yarangas started to hive into view, Armagirgin saw a whiskery lakhtak face just ahead. The big bearded seal had popped almost entirely above the water—only its flippers were hidden—and observed the boat with undisguised curiosity.

Armagirgin felt his blood beginning to boil. He unhooked the two nerpa, which sank immediately, and paddled over to the lakhtak, who responded by diving. Only ripples remained.

Armagirgin spat, furious, and paddled slowly to the place he thought the lakhtak would surface.

The creature came up so close that Armagirgin jumped. It gave Armagirgin a cheeky look and, just as mockingly, with exaggerated languor, disappeared into the deep. Armagirgin had time to clearly see the gray body undulating down and away.

Now he was really in a rage. He was almost prepared to jump into the water, in pursuit of this seal who dared laugh at him.

Once again he made his way to the place the seal would likely emerge. As soon as the whiskery head appeared, Armagirgin reached down and grabbed it with both hands . . . only for the seal to slide easily from his grasp and make a swift, forceful dive.

Armagirgin cursed and readied his harpoon.

This time, the seal surfaced a good deal farther from the

kayak. But when the hunter threw, all of his malice went into it. The blade punctured the seal's skin. Gingerly, Armagirgin pulled on the harpoon line, careful not to damage the wounded animal further. The seal's eyes were huge and pleading, but Armagirgin only smirked nastily and sang the louder as he rowed for home. The kayak was moving so fast it raised foam in its wake.

As usual, there were people waiting on the beach to meet the hunter. They cried out encouragement, praising his skill and luck. Armagirgin hauled the lakhtak to shore and, as the villagers dragged it out of the water, instructed: "Don't finish him yet!"

With these words, he sprang from the boat and fell on the seal, wielding his sharp knife. He skinned the creature, along with a layer of blubber, alive. The people had never seen such a thing before, and no matter how much they respected and feared Armagirgin, now they stood speechless and horrified.

The poor lakhtak was a bleeding wound all over. Laughing maliciously, Armagirgin raised the seal over his head and tossed him, flayed, back into the sea.

"Go on and tell your sea gods how strong and great is Armagirgin!" the hunter shouted. "Pass along the stupid tale that our old crazy Nau loves to tell!"

He stopped and looked about.

"Where is she? Why did she not come to the beach?"

"She's ill," someone replied.

"Ill?" Armagirgin furrowed his brow. "She's supposed to be immortal, isn't she? She's never ill!"

It was true. No one could recall seeing old Nau ill. But today she really was; she would not leave her yaranga.

The flayed lakhtak floated away from the shore, leaving a bloody trail in the clear, bright water.

The sun was fast disappearing beyond the horizon. From the untroubled sky there suddenly came fierce winds and heavy clouds. The calm surface of the water grew pockmarked, and no sooner had the people climbed up to their yarangas than the first big wave crashed thunderously onto the beach.

Coastal weather can be changeable, breaking unexpectedly, but this was unprecedented. A gust of wind tore several yaranga roofs clean away. A large skin bucket hurtled past a row of kayaks lashed to their struts. Garlands of drying walrus intestines took wing, flying far out into the lagoon. It was as though the mild summer's day had never been: the air itself darkened, and a soaking downpour cascaded from the low, bulging clouds.

People shouted as they tried to tie down flapping yaranga coverings; children wailed and dogs howled; these sounds mingled with the baying wind and rumbling waves. For good measure, bolts of lighting cleaved the gloom.

"*Ilkei! Ilkei!*" the villagers screamed, terrified.

Fiery arrows crackled through the sky, briefly illuminating the yarangas' smoke holes.

Armagirgin, huddled inside his home, sat clutching the handle of a ceremonial tambourine, willed to him by his grandfather Givu. He tried to dredge up some of his new songs, but instead there came unbidden the old, familiar words he had grown up with, words for addressing the sea, the animals, and his kinsmen. What were they, these words of kindness and love?

Leaving behind the tambourine, Armagirgin crawled out of his yaranga and, crouching low against the wind, clutching at the ground to steady himself, went to the yaranga where old Nau lay sick.

"Oh, it's you," she said weakly.

"What's happening?" said Armagirgin. He was truly frightened. "Is this all because of what I did to that lakhtak?"

"This is only a warning." Nau's voice was faint and frail. "The storm will pass; it can't go on forever. But you must look at yourself and see your actions with a different set of eyes."

"What kind of eyes?"

"The eyes of Great Love."

Armagirgin fell silent: from infancy he had heard these words, yet even now, in the midst of lightning flashes and the storm's roar, he doubted.

"What should I do, then?" he asked.

"Live according to your conscience," Nau told him. But Armagirgin didn't understand her words.

"How's that?" he said.

Old Nau just raised herself up on one elbow and looked at him in disbelief.

اﻟﻠﮫ

When he left Nau, Armagirgin found himself in a strange and unfamiliar state of uncertainty. On the one hand, he could see that his actions had called down the wrath of nature, and therefore the storm. But on the other hand, it wasn't the first storm they'd ever seen . . .

Giant waves rolled over the narrowest and flattest parts of the spit. The people from the sea-facing side had gathered up their belongings and, bending low under the weight of these possessions, were running for the relative safety of the lagoon side, where the waves had not yet reached.

Armagirgin barely made it back to his own yaranga. The sea had pulled down the outermost side already, and foamy brine sloshed about his chottagin. The hearth was flooded, starfish and shreds of seaweed jumbled with ash. Another wave rolled in, and with it came a little walrus pup, his tusks only beginning to grow in. He paddled his flippers comically, trying to find purchase, and plaintively blinked his eyes, nearly hidden in thick folds of skin. An ordinary walrus pup—except for his bright-red hide, which seemed to burn from within. The next wave washed the pup back into the sea.

The wind began to die down toward morning, and Armagirgin ventured outside. The wind was still wild enough to make the sea look as if it were boiling. Vast waves glowed as they rose high above, reflections from their crests casting an eerie gleam that seemed to reach all the way back to the horizon. Silent and chastened, Armagirgin went back to his yaranga.

3

After the great storm, when the yarangas were almost washed away, old Nau took a turn for the worse. It was a change everyone could see. She had always been old, but she had also been strong. Now she seemed deeply ancient. Her vision seemed to be going, too; she couldn't tell people apart and often gave confused answers. The only thing she remembered clearly and was always happy to tell was the well-worn fable of the coastal people's whale ancestry.

Whenever she began, in her reedy voice, the story of how once she was young and living a strange existence all alone, of how joyfully she wandered barefoot over the soft grass of the tundra, ready for Great Love, which then appeared to her in the guise of a whale, people struggled to conceal their derision. No one stopped the children from teasing the old lady openly. There were more important things to think about.

Life had grown harder. Nowadays, as often as not, the first frosts found meat pits only half-full. In the cracking cold of winter, people were forced to range far and wide in search of seals or polar bears. In the evenings, by scant firelight, they thought back on the good times when the shores teemed with life, and the hunt was more of an entertainment, a way for young men to test their mettle, than hard labor.

Rekken came several more times to the Shingled Spit, bringing disease. There was no one now to find them wandering and help them get clear of the village, so many people died, and the path to Funerary Hill never stayed snowed in for long.

Armagirgin did not spare himself. He went out on the ice at the first glimmers of sunlight and stayed out far into the night.

But usually he came back empty-handed. The sea was crusted in impenetrable ice, with no wind to break it up.

There were bear tracks on occasion, and Armagirgin soon realized that if you followed the great predator's footprints you just might find a half-eaten nerpa carcass. In the time before, bringing home such a thing was considered both sacrilegious and highly humiliating. But when you have ravenous kids and your own stomach is knotting with hunger, beggars can't be choosers.

He followed the bear's tracks now. They were clearly visible in the snow, and blue, brimming with the very color of the dark winter sky, the glittery stars and the rainbow shards of the polar lights.

The frost sliced through his lungs and wicked away the last vestiges of heat from his body. Armagirgin deliberately slowed his breath, conserving his energy, and adopted a long but unhurried stride. The bear had chosen a level path, skirting ice hummocks big and small. His tracks were unbroken, and this made the hunter wary: if the bear was without a kill, he would have nothing to share.

Armagirgin was ready to give up the chase when he saw the bear. The *umka* had climbed a small hummock and was standing upright, watching the human approach. He was unperturbed, sure of himself and his own strength. His slightly pointed face, with its black-tipped nose, seemed almost to be mocking the weak and hungry man.

Armagirgin felt his temper flare. He was on his own, without a helper to distract the beast—the way the umka was usually hunted—but so what? Why shouldn't he take on the bear?

The bear, however, seemed unwilling to do battle. He climbed down unhurriedly and loped away, shuffling the dry, powdery snow aside with his wide paws as he went.

Spear aloft, Armagirgin rushed the bear. The animal looked back at the source of the noise and his impassive face finally registered surprise. He halted and turned.

Armagirgin drew close and, with all his might, stabbed the point of the spear under the bear's front paw, where the heart lay. The bear gave a humanlike groan and fell, breaking the shaft. His eyes still flickered with surprise, but soon enough the fog of death had extinguished them.

Armagirgin stood over the fallen beast for some time, coasting on a huge, hot avalanche of pleasure and pride. Finally, he could hold it in no longer. He shouted wildly into the world, and his booming voice rebounded from the sharp edges of the ice hummocks and filled the deserted white expanse.

"I alone killed the umka! My hand drove the spear, and here he lies, the lord of the ice, defeated! Anyone else want to come at me from the sea? Anyone else to test their arm against mine?"

He shouted these words again and again. Finally, he got down to butchering the dead animal; in this kind of weather, you had to work fast. Once the carcass had stiffened, no knife would be sharp enough to cut through it. As he worked, Armagirgin lobbed chunks of still-warm meat into his mouth, sating his hunger, and his body flushed with the thick warmth of bear's blood.

He took as much meat as he could shoulder. The heavy load felt light to him because it was meat he carried—it was life, the promise of plenty, of good sleep, of an assured future. It was the glad proof of his power.

He was met by the kinsmen and neighbors who had sighted him from afar, knowing from the way he walked, with his burden on his back, that it was a bear he'd killed; he would have simply dragged a nerpa. They met him with cries of delight. He tersely gave the precise location of the rest of the bear carcass, and the strongest and fleetest youths hastened to retrieve it.

The women set up big cauldrons over their fires, and by dawn, when the meat was boiled, the most respected and important villagers were summoned to Armagirgin's yaranga.

"Don't forget Nau," he said.

So the old woman came, too, her haggard visage all but obscured by gray tangles of matted hair. The skin of her hands put Armagirgin in mind of a rain-battered walrus-hide overshirt. For an immortal, she certainly seemed to be aging by the minute!

Nau settled beside a blazing brazier, where it was warmer and smelled more strongly of fresh cooking. "Fortune has come to you," she addressed the hunter, quietly.

Armagirgin preened. "I grabbed it with these two hands!"

"That's right," nodded old Nau. "Fortune comes to strong hands."

"And to those who know themselves to be masters of their own fate," added Armagirgin.

"That's right, too," she agreed. "But to live life wholly, we must also love one another, love our brothers, and not just ourselves."

"Again with your old nonsense," laughed Armagirgin. "Better we get to eating already!"

The women entered with a long wooden dish, filled with steaming, smoking umka meat, which they set before the gathering. Everyone set upon the food, and for some time only the loud lip-smacking of the eaters and their moans of satiety broke the silence inside the spacious polog of the strongest and luckiest man on the Shingled Spit.

As their bellies filled, their tongues loosened. People began to reminisce about the days when hunting was plentiful, longing for summer, when there would be plenty of walrus meat and none of the cold, hungry nights of winter.

"It's going to be a hard summer," said Nau. She dropped a small bone, picked clean, back onto the empty wooden dish.

"How would you know that?" Armagirgin challenged.

"I just know," she told him calmly.

"Who told you?"

"I know it myself," returned the old lady. "Why should I listen to anyone telling me?"

Armagirgin gave her an appraising look. "Give us a foretelling, then, so we may have better luck."

"You should have thought of that before," Nau said. "You have to love not just yourself, but all people, and to love them unselfishly. You didn't call your guests here today because you wanted to share meat with them, did you? No, it was only your desire to boast, so that everyone could see and know it—here am I, Armagirgin!"

"Well, even if that's so, it isn't any of your concern!" he said crossly. "Your concern is to tell tales, not to teach people how they should live."

"Fine, I'll tell you another tale," said Nau, unruffled. "Listen ..."

"Oh, what's the point of listening to you, anyway?" Again Armagirgin dismissed her. "Even the little kids know all of your stories already. Stories of a life that is long past."

"I'll tell you a story of the future ..."

Suddenly wary, Armagirgin gave a condescending nod. "All right. Now our stomachs are full, why not a story?"

Nau made herself comfortable and began, in her throaty voice: "Every tale begins with the words 'This is how it was.' This story begins differently—with the words 'This is what will be.' This is what will be, then. There will be born a man, luckier and stronger than you, Armagirgin, though his name will be different. He will best the stoutest and fattest creatures of the sea, catch the fastest on land, and with his bare, mighty hands will be able to strangle wolves and bears. Far and wide, people will praise him and even make up tales and legends of his doings.

"But it will not be enough for him that people can see his glad face when he is in front of them; he will wish to be present always, in each and every yaranga. Skilled carvers will cut his likeness from walrus tusk, and his image will be painted onto white hides and hung from high poles. He will wish, too, that his very smell be present in every yaranga, and will order people to sniff him whenever they meet him, and will fill yarangas with his scent.

"But this will also not be enough. He will be clothed in the newest and best garments, but these will not do for him, and so the most accomplished embroiderers will decorate his clothes, and he will shine like the sun's twin. . . . Yes, and they shall liken him to the very sun, too, but even this will not be enough for him. He will desire that real stars be brought to hang from his clothes, and will send people to gather them, and these people will perish on their journeys. And he shall be left all alone then, and the shore will be wild and deserted, just as it was when I first came here, young . . ."

Nau's tale was finished, and she fell silent. Everyone else was silent, too, for there was much that was baffling in the old woman's words.

Armagirgin gave a wide yawn. "Time to sleep, I think. Now that we've eaten well and heard old Nau's tale, what more can we want but a long, sweet slumber?"

And with that, everyone returned to their own homes.

4

By spring, things were bad indeed: people were reduced to scraping down the walls of the meat pits, soaking and boiling up lakhtak-skin straps, and rooting for withered greens under the snow. Many starved, especially the babies who vainly tried to draw milk from their mothers' thin breasts, dried up like winter mittens.

Against expectations, the warmth of the returning sun did not cause the sea ice to break. It was only by the time the birds reappeared that a few melt holes formed and hunters began to have more luck.

Yet it was nothing like the plenty of yesteryear. Something had changed in nature, and no one could explain it—except old Nau, who insisted it was all to do with human greed and foolishness, with people's lack of respect for one another, for nature, and for all the other living creatures on sea and land.

The villagers, exhausted and hungry, could only shrug and roll their eyes at the senile old lady's pronouncements. Everyone knew that nerpa would never go to a hunter of their own accord, nor birds seek to entangle themselves in nets to please the trapper.

No, fortune favored those who did not stint in their efforts, spending days and nights out on the ice.

ﻋﻠﻢ

When the ice finally broke, life became a little easier. Men hunted in large seagoing canoes, sneaking up on walruses as the herds moved from the southern to the northern waters. The hunters would lie in wait, harpoon them, and drag them ashore, where the women stood ready with sharp knives. Fires burned in the yarangas, and once more the smell of boiled meat spread across the village, cheering men's hearts and inspiring glad songs in praise of Armagirgin, the man who had challenged nature.

Spring was a time of eating to make up for the ravages of winter, and it wasn't just seal and walrus meat. The villagers had discovered that bird eggs were exceedingly delicious, and so were the birds themselves—and it was easy to catch them, in big deer-tendon nets.

On still, quiet evenings, the villagers pillaged the shallow streams, scooping up somnolent fish. They found that the little blue flowers, when mixed with nerpa fat, went down a treat. In short, they experimented with anything edible, catching up after the ravages of the long hungry months. Lakhtak and nerpa ribs lay drying atop yaranga roofs, and when the meat dried and blackened, and white grubs could be seen to appear, they made the best eating. Seal flippers could be stowed in warm, close places, then after a while skinned and cut up into small pieces— the process gave the flesh an unusually sharp flavor, like needles on the tongue.

Food became not just a way to recover spent energy, but an object of pleasure—beyond satiety, to the tasting of delicacies. Someone had the idea of stuffing cleaned walrus gut with chopped-up hearts, livers, lungs, and gut fat, and braising the lot over a low fire. . . . The people of the Shingled Spit were in the grip of a mania.

Yes, now people ate well, perhaps even better than in the famed years of plenty. But there was a kind of uncertainty, too, in their gluttonous haste to fill the belly. A kind of dread.

They ate everything that could be got but did not manage

to store much away. When hard weather came, they would have to scrape together the last of what remained, then live by fishing. Finally they would tighten their belts and screw up their patience to wait for the wind to die down, making it possible to hunt passing walrus herds.

The waters of the Shingled Spit did not swarm with creatures as they once used to. There were no nerpa faces in the water or lakhtak bobbing up like curious children. No birds dashing about, no walruses bathing in the surf. Every living thing had gone, swam away, flown off. It was as though the animals had heard, somehow, about the insatiable greed of the villagers and took themselves elsewhere. And the people of the Shingled Spit really were insatiable, no matter that they of all the coastal folk were the stoutest, barely able to fit inside their own hide boats. They even spoke less, their mouths more often occupied with chewing on something or other.

Meanwhile, the short summer was coming to an end, and the walrus breeding grounds—where the villagers always got their winter provisions—lay drearily empty. Only the foamy surf came to play with the bare and spotless shingle. It rolled about broken walrus tusks, detritus of previous hunts; it slurped up shattered seashells and retreated, hissing, back to the cold, nearly deserted sea.

Only the whales stayed true to their native shore. Their pods continued to line the horizon, spouting sun-bright jets high in the air.

Rowing home in his empty boat, Armagirgin watched them with unconcealed hatred. He gazed at their smooth, giant bodies slowly descending into the deep and thought about their vast carcasses, treasure troves of meat and blubber. Why should anyone believe old Nau's preposterous stories of his people's ancestry? Why should whales be his forbears, rather than walruses or seals? If anything, seals looked a lot more like people, especially when they lay on the ice, looking up at the hunters. It was the resemblance that often did in a seal—a creeping hunter would imitate its movements, and the whiskery lakhtak would mistake the hunter for one of its own kinsmen . . . and at that, why not have wolves for ancestors? Wolves live on dry land and eat flesh, like humans. Who knew what these gigantic mounds of meat and blubber ate? All anyone knew was that it did not seem to include seals or walruses.

No, if you thought about it seriously, humans and whales were nothing alike—and that was why no one really paid any mind to the old woman's ramblings.

These were Armagirgin's thoughts, and with each passing day they grew more pressing. Eventually he shared them with the others. As it turned out, they had long thought the same as he did. As for old Nau's tales—well, there were lots of stories about human-seeming animals, tales of crows that spoke the language of men, of walruses singing songs, of foxes building yarangas . . .

For a little while longer, something held Armagirgin back. There was still the occasional walrus or seal to be caught, and people were not yet starving. Or perhaps it was old Nau. She was so weak that she no longer left her yaranga; she barely ate and never raised her voice above a whisper. Again and again, she spoke of giving birth to baby whales, who were brothers to all the living people. But no one paid her words any heed now.

That autumn the Shingled Spit saw an uncommonly large gathering of whales. They roamed very near the surf line, dousing onlookers in rainbow drops of water.

Armagirgin was hoping the walruses would return to their former colony beaches; there was even yet time to lay in a store of meat and blubber for the winter. But the beaches were empty. The walrus herds did not just avoid these places; they cut a wide, cautious berth around them in the water too.

Whenever he passed a pod, Armagirgin would mentally size up one whale or another, picking out the most vulnerable places on their bodies. He made long spears and took his friends off to the tundra, where he kept a dummy of a whale made from sod and mud.

Returning from the tundra one day, he heard old Nau moaning as she lay within her yaranga. He stuck his head inside the chottagin.

She seemed to recognize him. "Are you sick?" he asked her, feigning concern.

"It's bad," she whimpered. "There are times I feel like a spear is piercing me."

This was disconcerting. Could it be that his spear throws came to rest in the old woman's body? But that was impossible! Incredible! Maybe someone had told her of Armagirgin's secret training, and she was trying to warn him off?

علم

Some whales were still gathered nearby, so close that you could see them from the beach. This was the last remaining pod, the one to whom they had paid homage and made sacrifice in previous years. The whales seemed to be waiting for this customary gesture of farewell, and they headed toward the shore as soon as they spotted the boats' launch.

Suddenly, with an apparent premonition of danger, they banked sharply and headed for the open sea. The hunters gave chase.

"Spear the one at the back!" shouted Armagirgin. He was the first to throw his spear, piercing the skin of a young whale. First blood sprayed and colored the water, and other spears followed. But the whale was not vanquished yet. He launched himself after his companions, while the pod, as one, hastened away from the humans who chased them.

Armagirgin raced ahead and cut the young whale off from the rest of the pod. Spears outfitted with sealskin buoys rained down on the wounded creature. The buoys prevented the whale from diving; spent and weak from blood loss, he slowed. Blood poured from his many cuts, and the sight of it was intoxicating to the hunters. Each man tried to get a stab in.

The whale made one last attempt to rejoin his pod, but boats full of screaming, oar-waving humans barred his way. He stopped, seemingly resigned to his fate, and they finished him off in the water and lashed his lifeless body to the boats.

A rising wind filled their sails, and the victorious flotilla headed home.

It was a long trip. Night had fallen over the beach, and in the deep darkness, the hunters could barely tell one another apart. There was not a star in the sky, and even the moon did not appear. Proud Armagirgin sat at the stern of the lead boat and steered with a long oar.

They were met with joyful cries at the beach. Armagirgin ordered everyone back to their homes. "We'll butcher the whale come morning," he said tiredly.

Passing old Nau's yaranga, he heard a moan. Armagirgin went to lift the deerskin over the entrance.

Fixing her burning eyes on his, old Nau spoke hoarsely: "Today you have killed your brother merely because he does not look like you. Tomorrow, then . . ."

Her head dropped back. The eternal woman was no more. The woman of legend, who had outlived everyone and outlasted death itself . . .

ﻋﻠ

Early in the morning, with their sharply honed knives, the men descended to the beach to begin the work of butchering the whale. Armagirgin strode in the lead, staring straight ahead with keen, wide eyes.

But where was the whale? Where was the huge pile of meat and blubber that only yesterday they had hauled from the sea? Armagirgin ran down to the water's edge. The sea lapped at something there, small and hard to make out at first.

There was no whale. Instead, a man lay in the surf. He was dead, and the waves riffled his long, black hair.

Far ahead, to the very join of water and sky, the vast, empty sea stretched bereft of any sign of life or a single spout.

The whales had gone.

TRANSLATOR'S NOTE

I first "met" Yuri Rytkheu in the fall of 2004, over the phone, so early in the morning that it was still dark in London, and the day just beginning three hours ahead in Saint Petersburg. I'd been told he was an early riser and preferred the phone over email, and mornings to everywhen else. So I bought a calling card and collated my queries, and phoned. *A Dream in Polar Fog* was to be my first published translation, and I was getting cold feet.

We talked; we ran through a list of questions, mostly to do with small inconsistencies of the sort "three men get into a boat, four men get out." Earnestly, I asked about a few sentences that seemed to contradict themselves, and vocabulary that seemed oddly (but perhaps deliberately?) repetitive and didn't quite sound right in English. I wanted to be faithful to the book and was wary of editing out something meaningful that I'd simply misunderstood; but I was also keen to iron out irksome snags that were a product of lax editing and was curious to hear Yuri's views on being translated—by no means for the first time, though for the first time in English. Chuckling, he told me to iron away. Then, growing more serious, he said, "Don't worry too much about being exact. It's not a textbook. I want people to enjoy it and lose themselves in the story." And then: "Write it like a song. Like you could sing it if you wanted to." We were strangers, in most ways, and so I couldn't tell for sure whether it was a request or an instruction. Perhaps it was simply a benediction.

Months later, after a long dinner launching the book in Las Vegas—of all the unlikely places—as we trekked companionably down the endless corridors of the Mandalay Bay Resort and Casino, I finally got the nerve to ask him straight-out whether he liked the translation. Fluent in English but impervious to ambush, he only grinned. But later, as we headed for different airport gates, Yuri gave a me a hard-to-interpret look and then said, quite soberly: "In English, too, it sings. Let's do more books."

ﷺ

Uelen—which also appears in *A Dream in Polar Fog* and *The Chukchi Bible*—is the modern name for Yuri Rytkheu's birthplace, where Nau and Reu's yaranga once stood, all those generations ago. The topography of the Chukchi homeland includes cliffs, crags, plains, mossy and dry tundra, and all manner of ice and snow—not to mention a row of wind-lashed yarangas improbably lined up on a narrow sandspit between an ocean and a lagoon. A look at the map will prove more enlightening than a dictionary of Chukchi words. It is an astonishing landscape, geographically within sight of Alaska across the narrow Bering Strait, and yet inarguably perched on the outer rim of the world.

When the Whales Leave is a story concerned with ecology. The great lesson it teaches is that no human is outside nature, and the blind urge to consume and dominate is an expression of weakness, not strength. The best place in the world—though it may be harsh and unforgiving—is one's own homeland, and it ought to be cherished. The deeply spiritual commingles with the utterly practical, and kinship does not apply solely to men, but to all living things. Not until the closing pages of the novel, and many generations in, does the very first murder—the killing of the whale—occur. By contrast, the Edenic state of the Old Testament scarcely lasts two generations before degenerating into fratricide.

It is also a story of storytelling. Lived truth becomes a commandment, and then a fireside tale; memory becomes myth and is eventually relegated to an inconvenient fiction, given time enough. All stories end—even that of the first mother, who will be called the Always Living, many centuries after her death.

علم

Unsurprisingly for the founding myth of a people so intimately aware of and dependent on ice, water, and sun, not much happens in *When the Whales Leave* without a precise and detailed setting out of the weather conditions. Once again, I am indebted to the truly invaluable resource of *Encyclopedia Arctica* and its "Glossary of Snow, Ice, and Permafrost Terms" (found in volume one of a fifteen-volume reference work dating 1947–51), hosted online by Dartmouth College. There are many kinds of ice and snow, and the *Encyclopedia Arctica*, though unpublished, is a treasure trove of them, with helpful equivalents in several languages.

It is easy to form an impression of darkness and cold when reading about life at the edge of the world and the limits of human endurance. All good things—food, light, human tenderness—are associated with warmth. And yet—though wind is mentioned forty times, the word "snow" sixty times, and "ice" over seventy times—the most welcome weather word, "sun," appears in the book nearly a hundred times. Perhaps more appropriately still, for these descendants of whales, the nearly fifty instances of the word "sky" and the nearly ninety of "earth" or "land" are easily vanquished by the several hundred appearances of "sea," "waves," and "water." For a still and silent vastness, this landscape is also wondrously rife with sound: creaking snow and moaning wind, whistling gophers and shrill birds, burbling streams and murmuring surf, thrumming tambourines and crisply chiming stars.

Ancient yet piercingly timely, by turns mystical and matter-of-fact, mysterious and simple, and with a very unusual woman at its heart, *When the Whales Leave* is not just an elegy for a vanishing world, it is a lesson in duty and hope, and a story against the dark, cold night. I hope for new readers, too, it sings.

YURI RYTKHEU (1930–2008) was born in Uelen, a village in the Chukotka region of Siberia. He sailed the Bering Sea, worked on Arctic geological expeditions, and hunted in Arctic waters, in addition to writing over a dozen novels and collections of stories. Several of his books were published in European languages. The English translation of his book *A Dream in Polar Fog* was a Kiriyama Pacific Rim Prize Notable Book in 2006. In the late 1950s, Rytkheu emerged not only as a great literary talent but as the unique voice of a small national minority—the Chukchi people, a shrinking community residing in one of the most majestic and inhospitable environments on earth.

ILONA YAZHBIN CHAVASSE was born in Belarus and, together with her family, immigrated to the United States in 1989. She is the translator of Rytkheu's novels *A Dream in Polar Fog* and *The Chukchi Bible*, as well as the work of several other Russian authors. Educated at Vassar College, Oxford University, and University College London, she now lives in London with her husband and children.

ABOUT SEEDBANK

Just as repositories around the world gather seeds in an effort
to ensure biodiversity in the future, Seedbank gathers works of
literature from around the world that foster reflection on the
relationship of human beings with place and the natural world.

SEEDBANK FOUNDERS

The generous support of the following visionary investors
makes this series possible:

Meg Anderson and David Washburn
Anonymous
The Hlavka Family

milkweed
editions

Founded as a nonprofit organization in 1980, Milkweed
Editions is an independent publisher. Our mission is to
identify, nurture and publish transformative literature,
and build an engaged community around it.

milkweed.org

We are aided in our mission by generous individuals
who make a gift to underwrite books on our list.
Special underwriting for *When the Whales Leave*
was provided by the following supporters:

Mary and Keith Bednarowski
Phillip Hampton
William and Cheryl Hogle
Robin B. Nelson
Emily and Will Nicoll